TAKE THE HIGH ROAD

The Last of the Lairds
by
Michael Elder

SCOTTISH TELEVISION
in conjunction with

MAINSTREAM
PUBLISHING

This book is published by
SCOTTISH TELEVISION
Cowcaddens
Glasgow G2 3PR

in conjunction with
MAINSTREAM PUBLISHING
7 Albany Street
Edinburgh EH1 3UG

ISBN 1 85158 082 4 (cloth)
ISBN 1 85158 081 6 (paperback)

Typeset by Mainstream Publishing.
Printed in Great Britain by Collins, Glasgow.

Chapter One
1958-1961
1

Sir Logan Peddie tucked Isabel's arm into his own and patted her hand encouragingly. Not that she needed any encouragement. He glanced sideways at her face, which was calm, happy and unworried. He nodded briefly to himself. It was a responsibility taking her up the aisle to her wedding, a responsibility which he regretted having to perform. But Isabel's father lay in some desert grave in Egypt, a victim of the victory at El Alamein, one of the ones who did not return, and the rhododendrons at Glendarroch House had never been the same since John Urquhart left in 1939.

The notes of the voluntary from the organ faded and after a second's pause the *Bridal March* began, and he and young Isabel Urquhart began the short walk up the aisle to the altar and when she came down again she wouldn't be an Urquhart any longer, but a Blair. Heads turned in the pews which faced the altar and those which faced the church entrance craned to see between the people in front. The church was crowded. Brian Blair waited nervously at the altar, his younger brother David beside him, Brian's mop of unruly red hair not at all contained by the Brylcreme he had evidently plastered over it.

Sir Logan delivered Isabel at the altar, patted her hand again and then released her and turned to the Big House pew, where Dorothy and Elizabeth were already sitting, along with Sarah MacPherson whose husband was waiting to perform the marriage ceremony.

He settled back with a grunt. He was getting old, he knew, and these occasions didn't help to make him feel any younger. He glanced round at the assembled faces of his people, feeling that familiar surge of paternal affection for them. Margaret Urquhart, Isabel's mother, looking happy for her daughter and sad for her absent husband. There were Malcolm and Sandra

Blair, the other two parents. Scattered through the rest of the church he picked out the Lachlans, Grace and Donald, with Dougal sitting fidgetting between them. No place to bring a twelve-year-old boy to on a lovely July Saturday, he thought. The lad would be better off guddling for a trout in one of the burns. A first-rate occasion to get away with a fish scot free when most of the staff of the Big House were here and not able to patrol the policies. There were Jock and Ina Campbell and their son, young Jack. He must have a word with young Jack. The lad was about to take his first voyage, he understood. It would be interesting to know where he was going and which line he was sailing with. Might be able to give the lad a wrinkle or two. . . .

The congregation rose to sing a hymn. Sir Logan had missed the announcement of which one it was, but the organ blasted into the introduction to *Immortal, Invisible*. He fumbled through the hymn book, trying to find the number. Not that he would be singing. He never did. Simply mouthed the words. Dammit, he knew his voice was dreadful and Dorothy always complained if he tried to take part. However, it would look better if he had the thing open at the right place and at least mouthed a word occasionally.

He found it by the time they were halfway through the first verse, cleared his throat as if he were going to join in, glanced round again and met Graham Ferguson's eye. Dammit, he didn't want that. Graham nodded, smiled and returned to the study of his hymn book. Maggie stood beside him, bawling her head off as usual, of course, and Sir Logan returned to the words, avoiding Graham's look.

> . . . *Thy justice like mountains high soaring above.*
> *Thy clouds which are fountains of goodness and love . . .*

Stirring stuff, this, he thought. Good-going tune to it, too. Get the young Blairs off to a flying start. Inevitable as anything, this marriage of course. Fore-ordained since the pair of them were born, really. Still. Good to give them a rousing send-off. He wondered what Dorothy had picked as a wedding present for them. Must ask her later. Whatever it was it would be good and useful. Trust Dorothy for that.

These were, after all, his people.

2

It wasn't that he really wanted to go, Peter Cunningham told himself, as he sat in the passenger seat of the MG and watched Charles Maxwell's hands on the steering wheel. He wasn't into fast cars as Charles was, especially ones which, although very powerful, allowed the winter wind to whistle through the gaps in the hood and the rain to drip down the back of his neck.

They accelerated past Turnhouse Airport on the A9. Charles, who clearly relished this sort of activity, was whistling at the wheel.

"You'll see," he shouted encouragingly over the roar of the engine. "The New Year Ball at Glendarroch is one of the social events of the calendar."

Peter didn't doubt it. But, like fast cars, another thing he wasn't really into was socialising with the landed gentry, even though the work which he and Charles and several other keen young men undertook in the august offices of Paterson, James and Rider, W.S., brought them frequently into contact with such people. It was simply that since his parents were spending Christmas and New Year with Aunt Deborah and Uncle James in Truro, he had been left on his own over the holiday period, and having experienced a lonely Christmas he was less inclined to spend a lonely New Year as well, and so Charles's invitation to accompany him to the Glendarroch New Year Ball had seemed like a good idea at the time.

The car roared through Winchburgh, the wheels hissing on the wet spray of the road, the afternoon already darkening into an early night. Charles switched on the headlights and the twin beams cut a swathe of light through the skeleton trees on either side of the road.

He knew nothing of Glendarroch beyond the fact that Charles's grandfather was an old mate of the owner, Sir Logan

Peddie. They'd fought together in the First World War, and Sir Logan, it seemed, was very generous in his invitations to the New Year Ball. It was some kind of status symbol with him through which he could impress the world with the solidity of his background and the permanence of his existence.

He closed his eyes and dozed gently as Charles, crooning the *Skye Boat Song* to himself, propelled the MG through the gathering dusk. . . .

And the house was all he had imagined it to be. Enormous and solid, turreted and Gothic, it would have made an excellent four-star hotel, but as a private residence it must have cost a small fortune in heating bills alone. The trouble was, he thought, as he changed in the room to which he had been assigned, it was obvious that only a very small fortune was spent on the heating. A large one might have made the cold bearable. But later that evening, as the lights and the glittering company and the food and the drink began to wipe away the effects of the long cold drive, he began to see things in a different light. Sir Logan himself was a fine-looking old buffer, still ramrod upright though he must have been approaching seventy, grey haired, grey moustached and talking exactly like Peter imagined a cavalry colonel would talk and clearly very aware that he looked his best in Highland evening dress. Lady Peddie, his wife, was charming and had been beautiful, welcoming the guests and making them feel at home with the minimum of fuss and bother. But perhaps it was the daughter who caused some of the deep chill to disappear. Very tall, very slim, Elizabeth bore a distinct resemblance to both her parents. And she had inherited the easy manner which high birth had accustomed them to. He danced with her once or twice and in the modern dances, as opposed to the Scottish ones, where there was a chance to talk at a reasonable length and at a reasonable pitch of voice, he found her conversation to be as easy and charming and intelligent as her appearance. And it was a relief to be isolated in her company, away from other high-powered guests with names like Lord and Lady Strathmorris and the MacAulays of Letir-Falloch.

At midnight Sir Logan made a speech, one which had

obviously been made with minor variations every year for a long time, reminding his listeners that they were now moving into the last year of the nineteen-fifties, that changes were taking place, but that the one thing which would never change would be the New Year Ball at Glendarroch House, a remark which was greeted with cheers and clapping as though to prove that this was the first and greatest social event of the year to come.

Peter smiled and applauded too, feeling slightly apart from the Strathmorrises and the MacAulays and the rest of them. It wasn't simply that he was almost the only man present who hadn't got a title and was wearing an ordinary dinner jacket, it was simply that the life these people represented was not his. Even Charles, who had brought full Highland evening dress with him in the MG and who had drunk not altogether wisely, took part in the enthusiasm, as though he too were an integral part of this world. Peter allowed his eyes to rove round the beautiful dark-panelled hall with the portraits and the stags' heads and the bright and colourful company as Sir Logan went on, feeling in some way isolated and apart until he caught Elizabeth's eye as she stood some distance away. She smiled at him, a gentle smile, which might almost have been apologetic, as though she understood his reserve and his alienation from this scene, and that she sympathised with it. He smiled back, raised his glass in a silent toast to her, and she responded with her own.

Well, maybe coming here hadn't been such a bad idea after all, he thought, and wondered whether, after the speech, he could ask her for another dance.

3

Brian found his father in the storeroom unloading packing cases.

"Congratulations, son," said Malcolm, straightening up and holding out his hand. Brian shook it and grinned.

"Thanks, Dad," he said.

Malcolm was a short, stocky man with a wrinkled face and grizzled hair. He sat down on an unopened packing case and invited Brian to join him on another.

"I just wanted to tell you about your first anniversary present," said Malcolm. "Now that you're an old married man, I've been thinking."

"Do the two things go together?" asked Brian.

"Not exactly, but the one helps the other," said Malcolm. "And what I've been thinking is this. It's time you took over the store."

Brian blinked in surprise.

"Take it over?" he stuttered. "But — but why?"

"Because I'm retiring," said Malcolm. "If I'm going to grow vegetables I'd better start doing it while I can still bend."

"You can grow vegetables and run the store at the same time," said Brian.

"It's all fixed," said Malcolm quietly. "David finishes at Aberdeen University this summer. We don't need the money any longer. I saw the factor yesterday."

"What did you want to see him for?"

"To make the arrangements. Your mother and I have taken the lease of the cottage Miss Marshall had. We move in next month. That'll leave the house here clear for you and Isabel. There's a big garden there, and it's needing full-time attention. Miss Marshall never looked after it properly."

"I don't know what to say —"

"Then don't say it. It's all done. You take over the shop and the post office with Isabel. Make your home here. That's as it should be. That's what I did when my father retired."

Brian's main reaction was one of gladness. Since their return from their honeymoon in London a year ago they had stayed with his parents in the house behind Blair's Store. Finding a separate home had not been easy, and he had thought when Miss Marshall died last week that he ought to go and see Old Mackinlay, the estate factor, about getting the lease. Now, it seemed, his father had beaten him to it.

He told Isabel the news over a meal that night in the Auchtarne Arms and she was delighted. He watched her face with a continued tenderness as she smiled in the light of the candle on the table.

"That's marvellous, Brian," she said. "Will they mind moving out of the post office house, do you think?"

Brian hesitated before replying. There had been something in his father's attitude and voice which had given him cause to wonder, but the news itself had submerged anything else.

"I don't think so," he said. "He seems to be dead set on growing vegetables in Miss Marshall's garden. We'll be smothered in cabbages and carrots."

"We could probably sell them and make a huge profit."

He laughed and poured her another glass of wine.

"It'll be nice to have the house to ourselves," she said. "I don't mean your parents haven't been good to us. They have. They've been marvellous. But — well — it's not the same as having a place of your own, is it? Especially —"

She broke off and began to trace a pattern on the tablecloth in front of her. Perhaps it was a trick of the candlelight but he thought she looked a little flushed.

"Especially what?" he asked.

She looked up at him, her eyes full of love and pride.

"Especially as there will be three of us early in the New Year," she said.

There was a ripple of surprise in the Auchtarne Arms dining-room as the young man with the mop of red hair suddenly leapt to his feet, picked up the woman who sat opposite him, whirled her round and kissed her soundly, but neither Isabel nor Brian noticed it.

4

"It's quite divine, isn't it? Look at the depth of colour in that field," said Angela, adjusting her glasses, peering closely at the picture and tapping her teeth enthusiastically with her catalogue.

Elizabeth nodded and strolled on. Angela was apt to get these enthusiasms which faded as quickly as they developed. By tomorrow she would have forgotten the picture and even the name of the artist whose exhibition they were attending. She had been exactly the same at school.

The gallery was fairly small and very empty. There were only about four other people there. Outside, the Edinburgh sunlight slanted across the wide pavements and glistened on the black railings of the areas.

Elizabeth stopped beside another picture, a riot of colour and movement which was inaptly described in the catalogue as *Still Life*, and she wondered what the artist had been thinking of to give such a picture such a name.

"Willie's got a sense of humour," said a voice beside her and she turned and recognised the man standing beside her.

"It's Peter Cunningham, isn't it?" she said, as if she hadn't remembered the name immediately.

"Guilty," said Peter and they shook hands. He held hers a fraction longer than he needed to. "And what brings you to Edinburgh, Miss Peddie?"

"Just a visit to an old school friend," she said, nodding at Angela, who was now examining the picture with her head to one side as though she were wondering if it had been hung sideways.

"She's right. It *is* hung sideways," said Peter. "I told you Willie has a sense of humour. The artist, you know," he added in response to her blank look. "I was at university with him."

Angela straightened up, spotted Elizabeth and strolled towards them.

"Have dinner with me tonight," said Peter, and she blinked at the suddenness of the invitation

"I don't know whether I'm free —" she began.

"Eight o'clock. The Aperitif. What do you say?"

There was no time for thought. Angela had almost reached them. She felt like a conspirator as she nodded briefly and said, "All right."

He smiled and she introduced Angela to him and they stood and talked for a few minutes before he made his excuses and left the gallery with one last backward glance at her as though to remind her of their — assignation was the word which immediately entered her mind.

If it was an assignation it was a very innocent and extremely pleasant one. The side room at The Aperitif was quiet, the service excellent, the food delicious and she found herself sitting opposite him, talking freely and easily, and it was difficult to believe that she had only met him once before, at the New Year Ball, and that they had had perhaps a total of a quarter of an hour's worth of conversation. She didn't remember afterwards much of what they talked about that night, but it didn't matter. The important thing was that before the meal was over and he drove her back to Angela's flat she found that she had asked him to visit Glendarroch again and that he had accepted.

He owned a two-year-old Ford Consul, nothing very smart or flashy. When he stopped at Angela's flat he came round and opened the door for her and he shook her hand and held it once again a little longer than necessary, but he didn't try to kiss her and for that she was grateful, because she was not yet sure what she felt. She knew it would take a while to sort out what her feelings were.

5

Graham Ferguson tied up the ferry and climbed laboriously on to the pier. He stood for a moment to recover his breath. He seemed to have to do that more frequently now, though it was difficult to be sure when every breath was something of a labour anyway.

The leaves on the trees were beginning to turn gold, yellow, orange and russet, and already one or two were beginning to fall, fluttering gracefully to the ground in the still September air.

He looked down at the boat with regret. The planking was beginning to spring, and here and there the paint was blistered. At Auchtarne that morning he had got the boatbuilder to have a look at it and give him a rough idea of what repairs might cost. The answer had shocked him. It had also helped him to make up his mind.

He plodded off the pier and braced himself for the slight rise in the path towards the cottage. Always at the end of the day this path seemed steeper than it had been in the morning.

"Is that you?" Maggie's voice came from the kitchen.

"Aye," he said, wondering not for the first time exactly what answer she expected to such a question.

He turned into the living-room, threw his oilskin jacket over the back of a chair and sank into his own at the fire, feeling the ache in his chest worse than usual.

Maggie came bustling through, clicked her tongue as she picked up the oilskin and took it to the lobby to hang on the hook where it belonged, before returning to set the table for tea with a great deal of disapproving clattering and banging. He watched her as she worked, wondering about her. She was not unattractive, he thought, though her manner didn't help. He wondered if that was his fault. Probably. If it hadn't been for him, she might have been happily married by now with a bouroch of bairns round her knee. Would that have blunted her sharp tongue and would she have been more concerned not to upset people by what she said than she was now? But she had, not without occasional grumbling, taken over the job of looking after him since Jenny had died ten years ago, wasting the best years of her life on this useless old hulk. . . .

"I'm giving up the ferry," he said, and she stopped with a couple of knives in her hand and turned to him.

"You're what?" she asked.

"I got an estimate. From Napier. For repairs. Two hundred pounds," he said, speaking in short phrases to give himself time for breath between them.

"Two hundred? That's daylight robbery!" she said. "Wait till I see him!"

"No. It's fair enough. There's a lot to be done. I'll be sixty-five next month. The winter's coming on. The boat won't last without money spent on it. So I'm giving up."

She stood staring at him and he could see the conflicting emotions cross her face.

"Oh, you are, are you?" she said. "And what are we going to do for money? How are we going to live? Can you tell me that?"

She was so uptight about it that he wanted to laugh but he felt the warning tickle in his lungs and he coughed. Once started it was difficult to stop. He sat forward, trying to ease the tightness, to control the cough, and she sighed impatiently and came and slapped him gently on the back. It didn't really help and he'd told her so often enough, but perhaps she felt that by this action she was sharing his burden.

At last the coughing eased and he sat back, closing his eyes and he heard her clicking her tongue.

"You rest," she said roughly. "Bide where you are, you hear me? Tea in five minutes."

She bustled out and he heard the angry clattering of pans from the kitchen. He smiled. In spite of being glad that he was giving up the ferry she was taking her frustration out on the kitchen utensils. Not on him.

But he knew what her basic worry was. If he gave up the ferry, what were they going to do for money?

6

"What are you thinking about, Peter?"

He reined in his horse beside her and tried to regain his breath.

"How beautiful everything is," he said. "The horses. The scenery. You."

She laughed delightedly.

"In that order?" she asked.

"I don't think you can form an order. They all go together."

And that was true. She sat on her horse as though she had been born in the saddle. He knew he was clumsy and uneasy on horseback and made a poor showing beside her. And as she sat there, her head thrown back, silhouetted against the pale blue October sky, she seemed an integral part of the landscape, as indeed, he thought, she was.

They cantered back to the home farm, stabled the horses and

then walked along the track to the Big House. She took his
hand and he allowed it to remain there, though the touch
disturbed him in many ways. He felt a sexual arousal, and he
knew that he had become dangerously fond of her. But he also
knew that tomorrow he would be returning to Edinburgh and
the thought filled him with a return of enthusiasm and
something of relief. . . . That Melville case should be through
now, and he was already allowing his mind to wander
intriguingly around the question of whether a charge of
hamesucken would be allowed nowadays. He would have to
check when he got back.

And there would be escape. All through these two weeks, he
had been surrounded by a sense of expectation. From Sir
Logan, from Lady Peddie, even from Elizabeth herself and the
servants too. He could see the unspoken question in all their
eyes. When would he propose?

But he didn't. The next morning he threw his bags into the
Ford Consul and made a rather embarrassed farewell. Sir
Logan seemed stiff and formal. Lady Peddie was gracious but
cooler than she had been throughout his visit. And Elizabeth
looked hurt and bewildered, and he didn't like that. He waved
for the last time as the car turned the corner of the drive and the
laurel bushes cut off his view of her, and he felt an ache in his
heart. Damn it, he really had got very fond of her indeed.

He found that hamesucken wouldn't cover the Melville case.
It was true that Melville had broken into the plaintiff's house
and he had threatened him, but he hadn't actually assaulted
him, so hamesucken was out. Pity. It was such a lovely word...

But although working on that and other cases brought him a
feeling of belonging once again, there was something missing
now. It was a face and a body and a personality which kept
coming between him and the papers he was supposed to be
studying and which were growing daily into a stronger part of
him. He kept picturing Elizabeth swinging down one of those
narrow lanes, the hedges filled with the blackness of ripe
brambles, of Elizabeth galloping over the moors, her hair flying
loose and her cheeks flushed with the wind and the sun, until at
last he could bear this unaccustomed loneliness no longer and

one evening, after the rest of the staff had disappeared for the night, he reached for the telephone and asked the operator for the number of Glendarroch House.

She answered herself. He recognised the voice immediately and it brought him a thrill of pleasure and relief.

"Elizabeth? Peter," he said.

"Peter! How nice to hear from you. How are you?"

"Lonely," he said. "Will you marry me?"

There was a stunned silence and he wondered if he had been too precipitate, had jumped the gun too fast.

"Yes," she said. "But we'd better talk about it, hadn't we?"

"You bet we had," he said. "When can I see you? You don't know how I've missed you —"

"I've missed you too, Peter. Come this weekend. Can you?"

"Try to stop me. Friday evening?"

"Oh, Lord, as long as that? This is only Thursday!"

"Till tomorrow then. Oh. By the way. I love you."

"That's just as well in the circumstances, isn't it? And it also makes things easier, because I love you too. Tomorrow?"

"Tomorrow."

He put the receiver down slowly and wondered just exactly what he had done and whether he had been wise.

He wondered more over the weekend at Glendarroch. His reception was totally different from his departure. Sir Logan nearly pumped his arm off and kept referring to him as his dear boy. Lady Peddie kissed him tenderly on the cheek. And he kissed Elizabeth for the first time and it was good and exactly what he had expected and hoped for.

But then the worries. He was dragged round the village and the outlying crofts the next day by Sir Logan and introduced to everyone as Sir Logan's future son-in-law, and the implication which grew stronger with every call they made was that here was the new laird of Glendarroch, the man who would take over from Sir Logan when the old man finally joined in the graveyard the long line of Peddies who had owned Glendarroch before him.

It was impossible to protest in the presence of Sir Logan's people, impossible to tell him that this wasn't what he had in mind at all, that his life was firmly fixed in the offices of Paterson, James and Rider, W.S., in Edinburgh, and that was where he intended to stay.

The sooner he got Elizabeth away from all this, he thought, the better. It had all seemed so simple on the end of the telephone. Now he wasn't so sure.

7

The great thing about Syme was that he was a talker, thought Maggie as she sat on the other side of the kitchen table from him and listened to the torrent of words pour out of him while the rain poured down outside and lashed against the window and the wind roared through the naked branches of the trees in the blackness of the night. Maggie was pretty good at talking herself, but she couldn't hold a candle to Syme. Every blink of his children's eyes, every word Mrs Syme had said to him and he had said to Mrs Syme were carefully reported. The great thing was that you didn't have to listen because he never expected any response. You were free to pursue your own thoughts.

And Maggie had several of those, principal amongst them being, what was Sir Logan saying to her father through there in the living-room?

Syme was Sir Logan's chauffeur, and Sir Logan's Armstrong-Siddeley stood outside the cottage as Sir Logan's car had so often stood outside the cottage in the past. Unkind gossip in the village used to say that Sir Logan came to see Maggie, and her reputation on several occasions was nearly ruined by the maliciousness of the stories put about. It used to anger her, but not any more, she told herself. She and most sensible people knew that Sir Logan only came to see her father. The two of them sat for hours together, reminiscing about the old days during the Great War when her father had been Sir Logan's batman till that gas attack had had him invalided out. There weren't many of them left now. Last week at the Armistice service at the village war memorial she had counted only six. Every year there were less. It was the younger ones, the ones who had fought in the Second War who were in the majority now, men and women joining together in remembrance of fallen comrades, of, let's face it, a time which now seemed a lot more exciting and meaningful than the present day. We are the ones in the majority now, she thought. The old ones from the First War are being gradually eased out, perhaps made less important as their numbers decreased. Well, if the old man was one of them the sooner the decrease happened the better.

The living-room door opened.

"Syme! We're off!"

Syme stopped in mid-sentence at the sound of Sir Logan's voice, grabbed his cap and hurried through to the lobby. Maggie followed and found Sir Logan shrugging himself into his waterproof.

"Good night, Maggie," he said. "Sorry, and all that. Think I've tired him out."

He clapped her on the shoulder and then hurried down the path to the Armstrong-Siddeley where Syme stood waiting in the rain and the wind at the open door of the car.

She closed the door as the Armstrong-Siddeley drove off, went into the sitting-room and looked at her father suspiciously.

"Well, what did you gossip about this time?" she asked as she gathered the whisky glasses and the bottle which Sir Logan had brought and which he had left half full on the table by her father's chair.

"This and that," he said vaguely. "But there is one thing, Maggie," he added and there was something in his voice which made her pause at the door and look round at him. "When I go, Sir Logan will see you right."

"Don't make me laugh. And it's time you were in bed," she said and hurried away to the kitchen to wash the glasses, wondering exactly why it was that Sir Logan would "see her right".

8

Brian realised that his ideas about what happened when a child was born must be sadly different from reality. He had always imagined that people ran around for hours with pans of boiling water, that it took a long time and that the doctor eventually appeared in his shirt sleeves, sweating and exhausted, to tell the husband that he had become a father.

In fact it all happened so quietly and so smoothly that he was scarcely aware of what was going on.

Isabel was washing the dishes that morning and he was drying them before going through to open up the shop. Isabel was very large now, but he had become used to it. She moved slowly and carefully as though slightly unsure of her balance and she had just made a joke about it being time he took over washing the dishes as she was beginning to find it difficult reaching them when she suddenly straightened up, put a hand to her back and supported herself on the edge of the sink for a minute.

"Brian, I think you'd better go and get mother," she said so matter-of-factly that it was a second or two before her real meaning sank in.

"It's starting?" he asked.

She nodded.

"I think so," she said.

Immediately he began to fuss around like a demented hen and she waved him away.

"It's all right. I'll go and sit down. It's probably a false alarm. Perhaps you'd ring Dr Wallace too."

He sped off, unwilling to leave her, but the Urquhart cottage was only a hundred yards down the road and he reckoned he was there in less than fifteen seconds.

Jean Urquhart had the Hoover going, but she switched it off and followed him back to the store without stopping for a coat, even though the January wind was sharp and the frost severe.

He rang the surgery in Auchtarne and young Wallace's wife said that one of the doctors would be with them within the hour, and it was after that that he began to feel helpless.

Isabel's mother had helped her up to bed and he sat downstairs, fidgetting, while he listened to the sound of conversation coming from up there, and the occasional laugh. It all sounded terribly normal and shouldn't have been frightening at all. And it probably wouldn't have been if he'd had anything to do. Like boiling water.

He moved restlessly between shop and living-room, serving customers, standing at the foot of the stairs listening.

Old Dr Wallace arrived and went straight upstairs and came down again in a few minutes and said he'd a few other calls to make and he'd be back at lunchtime.

That seemed terribly casual to Brian. He went on serving customers but his mind wasn't really on the job. People must have seen Wallace's car and word had got round because the shop was busier than usual. He managed to fend off questions and at one point during a lull he slipped upstairs and found Isabel in bed, quite comfortable, and looking perfectly normal.

"Stop worrying," she said. "*I'm* not."

"It's easy for you," he said. "You're only having the thing. I've got to stand around and watch."

She chuckled and then broke off as another pain took her, and he hurried out of the room, yelling for her mother who had taken the chance to go downstairs and make a cup of tea.

Wallace returned at lunchtime, by which time the pains were coming frequently.

He closed the shop for lunch and found he didn't want to eat anything. He sat alone in the living-room. The three were closeted upstairs and he felt useless. Nothing seemed to be happening.

Shortly after he reopened the shop Wallace appeared and beckoned to him. Maybe at last he was going to ask for boiling water. For the last half hour or so he'd actually managed to forget about what was happening upstairs.

"Congratulations, Brian," said Wallace. "It's a boy."

He held out his hand and Brian clasped it in relief and gratitude.

"They're all right?" he asked.

"Fine. No trouble at all."

Brian became aware of the thin, high cry of a child from upstairs.

"There he goes," said Wallace. "Taking exercise already. Up you go and see them."

Isabel was sitting up, looking pale and considerably smaller than when he had seen her last, and he went and kissed her and said things to her which, through his relief and love for her, he couldn't afterwards remember.

"Meet your son," she said, and he turned. Beside the bed the little crib was now occupied. A tiny dark head lay still and he looked with wonder at the new life he had helped to create. Not that he could see much. Quite apart from the fact that the baby was so wrapped up, his eyes seemed unaccountably misty and he couldn't really focus properly at all.

9

"Miss Ferguson, come in. Sir Logan said I was to take you through as soon as you arrived. Would you like to leave your coat here?"

Maggie was surprised. When she'd rung Martin Mackinlay and asked for an interview with Sir Logan she hadn't realised that it was going to be as easy as this. Mr Mackinlay, of course, you could see at any time. He was a grand old boy, even she had to acknowledge that, but it wasn't easy getting past him to see Sir Logan.

She allowed him to relieve her of her coat and watched him as he hung it on a hanger on the back of his door. He was a round, dapper little man with a shiny bald head. He took her arm, propelling her firmly out into the stone-flagged corridor, along the passage to the green baize door, and through that into the front hall of the Big House, somewhere she had never set foot in before. He guided her across the hall, which seemed to consist of a sea of rugs, past portraits of ancient Peddies, to the door of the morning-room, which he opened, ushering her in.

"Miss Ferguson, Sir Logan," he said and closed the door behind him.

Maggie gulped as Sir Logan rose from one of the leather armchairs by the fire and came towards her, a copy of yesterday's *Times* in his hand.

"Maggie, my dear. Come in. Sit down. How's your father? Not any worse, I hope?"

She shook the hand which he held out to her and sat on the edge of the chair, wondering at the importance which he seemed to be attaching to her visit. To get past Old Mackinlay so easily and to be greeted by Sir Logan so affably, made her distinctly nervous.

"Just as much of a pest as ever," she said.

"Shouldn't say things like that, you know."

"Well, he is."

"Look after him well. He's a damned good man, Maggie."

She snorted impatiently and then covered the snort with a cough, remembering what she had come for.

"I was wondering, Sir Logan —" she began, and then stopped, suddenly shy at the enormity of her petition.

"Go on, my dear," he said encouragingly.

She drew a deep breath.

"The ferry finished three months ago," she said. "Folk are finding it difficult to get to Auchtarne now. We're cut off from the outside world."

"I know what you mean."

"I've been asking around. There's a bus for sale at Duff's Garage in Auchtarne. It wants a wee bit of work done on it. I'd need to get permission from the council to run a service, but I thought —"

"You'd start a bus service between Glendarroch and Auchtarne?"

"Something like that, yes."

"That's a damned good idea. You mean you'd drive the thing?"

"Of course."

"And maybe your father could give you a hand, eh? Good for him to have something to do." She hadn't thought of that and wasn't sure whether she liked the idea or not. "Don't you need a — whatchamacallit — a special licence of some kind?"

"I've got that. I drove heavy vehicles at the end of the war."

"Then that's it. Damned fine notion, Maggie. First rate. Just what I'd have expected of you. See Mackinlay about the details."

"You mean, go ahead?"

"Of course I mean go ahead. Well done, Maggie. And any help I can give, let me know. You've got details of costs, outlays, all that sort of mumbo-jumbo?"

"Yes, I —"

"Give them to Mackinlay. I'll tell him to fix everything."

She left Glendarroch House in something of a daze. It had all been so easy. Sir Logan had treated her almost as a father would treat a daughter. . . . But then, she thought, in many ways he always had done. . . . Why? . . .

10

Brian locked the shop door, turned the sign to "Closed" and then went through to the living-room for his midday meal.

He was surprised to see Isabel sitting there with old Dr Wallace who was quietly drinking a cup of tea.

"Nothing wrong, is there?" he asked.

"Not a thing," said Wallace. "I was just passing and saw the pram outside. Thought I'd have a quick look at Jimmy. Isabel thought I was trying to kidnap him."

"Now, I never did," Isabel protested.

"Well, you appeared fast enough," said Wallace, twinkling at her. "He seems a pretty healthy specimen from what I was allowed to see before I was dragged unwillingly in here."

"He doesn't do anything by halves," said Brian. "He eats a lot, sleeps a lot and makes a lot of noise."

"Exactly what he should do," said Wallace. "No problems?"

"Well, yes," said Isabel. "Can you give Brian something to stop him from drooling over Jimmy?"

"I'm afraid that's incurable amongst fathers," said Wallace. "Though the condition can be eased."

"How?"

"Have another one. It helps to divide the attention."

Brian laughed.

"Well, we've been thinking about it," he said.

"I'm delighted to hear it."

"It's far too soon, don't you think so, doctor?" said Isabel.

"Don't drag me into it. Not yet, anyway. There are those who want a good long time between children so that they can get the messy bit over before they start again. And there are those who have them as quickly as possible to get the messy bit over in one prolonged awful messy bit. You take your choice." He got up and picked up his medical bag. "And now you'll need to feed your other man, Isabel, so I'll leave you to it. Nothing wrong with his appetite either, I hope?"

"It's not as big as Jimmy's but he's not far off it."

Wallace laughed and Isabel took him through to the kitchen to show him out by the back door. When she came back she found Brian sitting at the table with his knife and fork clutched expectantly in his hand.

"All right, woman, where is it?" he asked.

She cuffed his shoulder and then kissed the top of his head.

"Men!" she said. "My trouble is I'm outnumbered now."

"Maybe we should even things up a bit."

"I haven't the remotest idea what you're talking about," she said as she retired to the kitchen and began to clatter around with dishes, but Brian noticed before she disappeared that she was blushing.

11

The line seemed to stretch out to the crack of doom and Elizabeth began to feel that her smile had become fixed and false as she shook hands with all those who had attended her wedding. Her father had said it would be a day to remember, and it was certainly that. It was tempting providence to erect a marquee on the lawn of Glendarroch House as early as April but their faith had been rewarded with perfect weather, warm and sunny and windless. And everyone from the estate had been invited here. Her father had insisted on that, and now, after the ceremony in the tiny church which had been packed to the rafters came the really touching bit, receiving the good wishes of all those who were a part of the family of Glendarroch. They were kind and thoughtful, sorry she was leaving them to go to distant parts, for Edinburgh was like a foreign land to many of them, pleased that she had found the right man for herself, appraising Peter who was doing a splendid job beside her, being utterly charming and friendly and everything he should be. Then there was the other side of the coin. The neighbours and the other landed gentry. The Strathmorrises and the MacAulays. They had a separate table for the reception, of course. The only disappointing thing was the lack of Mr MacPherson, who had just married them. It had been brave of him to undertake the ceremony, but the reception would have proved too much for him. She thought of poor Sarah MacPherson's grave not yet grown over with grass in the kirkyard and turned her mind resolutely away. This wasn't really the time to be thinking of such things.

There was champagne by the bucketful, but she noticed, as did her father with a knowing twinkle, that many of the local folk slipped quietly away and came back with glasses filled with a liquid of a slightly darker colour and without bubbles.

Her father called for silence and began by saying, "I'm no hand at making speeches", at which in the anonymity of the crowd a few voices were raised in incredulous wonder and someone shouted, "Whaur's yer Hogmanay noo?" which was greeted with gales of laughter in which Dad took the lead.

"What I want to say is the usual sort of rubbish that's said on these occasions," he went on when the laughter had died down. "It's always said, because it's always meant, dammit. We feel we aren't losing a daughter. We're gaining a son. We may have lost the name Peddie this afternoon, but what's in a name, eh? I'm sure you'll all get used to Cunningham instead in a very short time. As you all know the idea of gaining a son is something which has always been very dear to Lady Peddie's heart and mine, and we welcome Peter to the family with our warmest good wishes. . . ."

She glanced at Peter, sitting next to her, and wondered about the expression on his face as her father went on to say that now they had a future laird when he himself finally packed it in, and people shouted "Shame!" and "Never!".

But Peter didn't look exactly joyful at the prospect, and she suddenly wished that they had spent a little more time talking about exactly what their future was going to be. She knew that to begin with they would go to Edinburgh and she would undertake the business of becoming an Edinburgh lawyer's wife, but they hadn't looked any further ahead to what would happen when the estate needed her which, she sincerely hoped, would not be for a long time yet.

But it was too late to talk about it now, and when she went into the house to change for going away, her mother came to her and hugged her with unaccustomed intensity.

"Have a son, my dear," she said.

"Good Lord, Mum, give me time," said Elizabeth.

"Yes, but not too much time. It's your father's dearest wish, you know. I didn't succeed in giving him one."

"That wasn't your fault. It's the father who decides the sex of the child."

"So they tell me," said her mother without much belief. "But you will, won't you? Then your father will know that Glendarroch is safe."

As Angela, her bridesmaid, fluttered around her, making sure that she had the right shoes on, she wondered guiltily whether anyone had thought of actually talking to Peter about how he felt about eventually settling here at Glendarroch, of taking over the job of running the estate, of becoming a father, not only, perhaps, to their son, but to all the people who lived on Glendarroch and who relied on the Big House for their existence. Probably no one had, because it was so much a part of their lives that it was difficult to believe that it wasn't a part of his, and she wondered whether that might not have been a mistake.

12

It was such a tentative tap on the back door that she knew who it was straightaway. Maggie muttered impatiently to herself and deliberately finished drying a dish at the sink before she strolled to the door and opened it.

Standing outside was the familiar small figure with the mop of mousy, receding hair, the ridiculous moustache, both hands clutching the cloth cap as though he were scared it would blow away.

"You again," she said.

"Yes, it's me, Maggie. I'm sorry —"

"What is it now?" she asked, not asking him in.

"There's something I wanted to tell you," he said.

"Then tell me."

"It's my Uncle Alex. You know, the one in Shetland. He died last week. It was a heart attack, but it wasn't really unexpected —"

"Get on with it!"

"Yes, Maggie. Well, he's left me his holding there, you see. A wee house and a couple of fields —"

"So you're off to Shetland now."

"Yes, Maggie. And I wondered if —"

"You wondered if I'd go with you, I suppose. Sorry Watson, you must be out of your mind. I wouldn't go to Shetland with you if it was the last place on earth, which it is, and if you were the last person on earth, which you aren't."

"I know, Maggie. I'm sorry. It's just that I thought if I sold it it might raise a wee bit of money for us and then we could maybe get married and you wouldn't say I was too poor any longer—"

"I've told you before and I'll tell you again, I'm not going to marry you. Can you not understand that?"

"Yes, Maggie, but I thought this might make a difference."

"Well, it doesn't. I've got my father to look after, you know, and that's a full-time job on its own. And now there's this bus service to get started. I've got plenty to occupy my mind without bothering about a wee whitterick like you."

She shut the door in his face and waited behind it until she heard the slow, disappointed footsteps withdraw round the side of the house. Then she returned to the sink, and promptly dropped a saucer on the stone floor where it smashed to pieces. She muttered a curse as she fetched a dustpan and brush and knelt down to sweep up the bits. Why did Sorry always make her so angry when he proposed, which he did regularly once every three months or so? It was extremely irritating, especially as it had been going on for nearly fifteen years, and she paused for a moment in her work as a new thought suddenly struck her. Was she wise to have sent him away like that? After all, she wasn't getting any younger.

13

Elizabeth made herself a cup of tea, took it into the sitting-room, and sank down into the armchair in the big bay window, kicking off her shoes as she did so. Children were playing in the park opposite. Their clear, high-pitched voices came through the open window along with a welcoming breeze.

She took a sip from the cup. Well, this and coffee would have to suffice from now on, and she laughed aloud at the thought. No more alcoholic beverages until the end of January. Fancy missing Hogmanay. Oh, well, there was always tomato juice.

It was funny that she couldn't yet feel the new life within her. When the doctor confirmed this afternoon that she was pregnant and that she might expect an addition to the family sometime towards the end of January, she felt somehow that she ought immediately to be made physically aware that what he told her was true. Of course, she already had the symptoms. Peter hadn't noticed her sickness in the morning. She had managed to conceal it from him, at least until she could be sure that it wasn't simply something she had eaten the night before which had disagreed with her. And it hadn't been all that bad or all that frequent either.

She sat back and closed her eyes, letting the warmth of the

news flood through her. She imagined herself telling Peter this evening when he got back from the office. She knew he would be delighted. . . .

The office. She wished she understood more of what he did there, could enjoy the company of his colleagues better. But she found when she met them that they were on a different wavelength to her, and though she did her best to understand their technical jargon and their in-jokes and their interest in the golf course or the rugby season, she found it impossible to do so. Often at a cocktail party when that sort of chatter was going on around her she found her mind drifting back to Glendarroch, to how the hills would be looking at the moment, recalling the sparkle of the sunshine on the loch from Laird's Point, all the dear familiar things which she missed more than she cared to admit. And then she would be brought back to the present by a remark aimed directly at her and she stammered and stuttered like an idiot because she hadn't been listening to what was going on around her.

On an impulse she got up and went to the telephone, dialled the operator and asked for trunks. She gave the Glendarroch House number and waited with that keen sense of anticipation while she heard the number ringing at the other end, feeling a little guilty because she was making this call without asking Peter. He wouldn't object, of course, but she felt such calls were expensive and something of a luxury.

It was her mother who answered.

"Mum? It's me — Elizabeth."

"Elizabeth? Why are you ringing just now? It's the expensive time. Is there something wrong?"

"No. There's something right. I wanted you to know straightaway. How would you feel about being a granny?"

There was a startled silence at the other end and then she could hear the relief in her mother's voice.

"Oh, Elizabeth, my dear, that's the most wonderful news. When is it to be?"

They exchanged all the important information, and Elizabeth felt tears in her eyes through her happiness as she spoke to that distant voice, picturing her mother standing there beside the telephone in the morning-room with its panelled walls and the view down the lawns towards the loch. She was probably wearing that old green tweed skirt and the twin set. . . .

"Your father will be delighted, darling. Now you look after yourself, won't you?"

"Of course I shall."

"When are you coming to see us?"

"Oh soon, Mummy. Very soon," she said. She used the diminutive form very rarely and only under the stress of extreme emotion and a little later the second set of pips caused her to say a hasty and unsatisfactory goodbye and hang up. She returned to the window seat, wiping her eyes and stood looking out at the children playing in the park, not seeing them, seeing instead the lawns and the trees and the loch beyond the morning-room window, and the roofs of the houses of the village beyond.

14

She had reckoned that fifteen passengers per trip would cover the costs. Any more would actually be profit. This morning there were seventeen passengers on the bus, and Maggie felt that things were beginning to look up. The service had been operating for a week now and there had been an increase each day. Thanks to Old Mackinlay, who had taken over the entire setting-up operation, the establishment of the bus service had been relatively smooth and well publicised. And it kept her and her father apart. He had willingly taken over the job of driving the bus occasionally to give her a break, and because of that and her own involvement in driving the thing they didn't have to spend so much time together. Which was a relief.

She turned the bus into the Auchtarne station yard and stopped. The people trooped off until she knew that there was only one left.

He came down the gangway and stopped at the driver's seat.

"I'm off, then, Maggie," he said.

"Aye, well, have a nice time," she said.

He looked at her with those sheep's eyes which irritated her so much.

"I wish you were coming too, Maggie," he said wistfully.

"Don't be daft. How could I? When will you be back?"

"I'm not sure that I'm coming back," he said.

"You mean you may bide in Shetland?"

"Well, there's nothing to come back for, is there?" he said sadly and she snorted.

"Away you go, Sorry Watson."

In the distance came the whistle of the approaching train and he nodded.

"Aye. I'll need to," he said. "Goodbye, Maggie."

"Goodbye, Sorry," she said.

He hesitated, made to say something, thought better of it, then heaved his old suitcase off the bus and carried it into the ticket office without looking back.

A little later the train panted into the station and there was a flurry of activity before there was a shriek from the whistle and she watched the black engine belch smoke as it drew the four carriages out of the station and up the incline into the cutting beyond. The signal clanged back to danger, the smoke cleared and the train was gone.

A few people boarded the bus, and a little later she began the homeward journey, feeling curiously empty as she did so.

Should she just have let Sorry go like that? Well, why not? He was an insignificant little man. He'd never make anything of himself. Never be worth a brass farthing. People would simply laugh at the idea of Maggie being Mrs Sorry Watson.

She wrenched the bus round a bend slightly too fast, and told herself to settle down.

And there was the additional worry which had been growing in her recently, ever since it had proved so easy to persuade Sir Logan to allow her to set up this bus run. Why had he done that? Why had he treated her as though she might be his daughter? Why had he taken this extraordinary interest in her?

Did it mean that she *was* Sir Logan's daughter? There were stories about him in his younger day. Lots of stories. And there were stories about the amount of time he spent at the

Ferguson's cottage.... My goodness, that would be something! Daughter of a fine upstanding gentleman like Sir Logan Peddie, rather than of a broken-down nonentity whom she had to nurse like a baby.

Was she, she wondered, really Maggie *Ferguson*? Or was she perhaps Maggie *Peddie*? If so, then the last thing she would want — or Sir Logan would want — would be for her to become Mrs Sorry Watson.

15

Money in the safe. Keys in his pocket. Ticket window shut and locked. Lights off in ticket office. Door locked. Check left luggage doors. Check waiting-room fire. Check gent's and ladies' lavatories for vagrants, etc.

The one thing Hector Mack didn't like checking was the ladies' lavatory, and he coughed loudly before he went in, but there was no one there.

He continued to check off the list of Things To Do in his mind. Having satisfied himself that he had done all but the last, he switched off the lights and then stepped out of the little ticket hall on to the dark platform and stood there with a feeling of unaccustomed power.

This was his domain. While Mr Purdie, the stationmaster, was on holiday, he was in charge of the station on the backshift. It was his responsibility to see that the work of British Railways went as smoothly as possible.

There was a bright moon shining high in the sky and it was late because the Glasgow train had been delayed for more than an hour down the line. He looked at the metallic reflection of the rails in the moonlight, the two sets through the station, joining into one at either end, and he thought of the miles of single line stretched out in either direction linking Auchtarne with so many other places all over the British Isles. Really, it was a tremendous responsibility he had at the moment.

He had earlier locked the buildings on the up side of the line, after the Glasgow train had left. Now the northbound train, delayed in the loop until the Glasgow train came through, had gone as well, and the station was silent and empty except for himself until the following morning when the early shift would open up in time for the first train and the business of the day would begin again, keeping the wheels of Britain's transport turning.

Close ticket hall door and lock. That was the final item on the list in his mind, and he dutifully unhooked the door and closed it, locked it and put the key safely in his pocket.

He heaved a little sigh. His responsibilities were over until his shift in the ticket office started again at midday tomorrow, and he felt sad at the thought.

He made his way to his motor scooter, and it was only as he reached it that he became aware of the fact that he was not alone in the station yard. There was a figure standing under the oak tree just at the edge of the road.

The station clock told him it was nearly midnight, which was not surprising. He had entered in the log the fact that the last up train had arrived seventy-one minutes late, but had left again after its requisite two-minute stop. It was very late and there was no sign of life around the station.

He gulped a little and wondered whether he could get the scooter started and reach sufficient speed to get past whoever it was standing at the entrance. But no. The figure was moving. It was coming towards him, and Hector's heart beat a little faster. There was a fairly heavy spanner in the toolbox behind the saddle. Now, if he could just get it out . . . but the catch seemed to have stuck and the more he struggled with it the tighter it seemed to get. . . .

"Excuse me."

It was a woman's voice and the sound of it brought a little relief. He turned slowly and saw in the moonlight a small, thin woman with straggly hair of an indeterminate colour, and a longish, youngish not very pretty face with dark appealing eyes.

"Can you help me?"

It was perhaps the first time in his fifty-seven years that anyone had asked Hector for help.

"It depends —" he said cautiously, because he suddenly

remembered that he had heard stories about bad women who cornered men at night and got them into trouble. Then they blackmailed them. . . .

"I was on the train from Glasgow and I thought the bus left from the square. Not the station. By the time I got back it had gone. And I have to be in Glendarroch tonight and I don't know how I can get there."

That sounded quite possible and the more he heard this person and the more he saw of her in the bright moonlight the less likely it seemed that she was a bad person who might have wicked designs on him.

"Glendarroch?" he said. "There isn't another bus till tomorrow morning."

"What can I do?" she asked, a note of desolation in her voice.

"You might stand at the road-end and perhaps someone might be going there who could give you a lift —"

"Oh, I wouldn't like to do that. You never know. It might be a bad man —"

The sudden echo of his own thought gave him an unaccustomed courage.

"It's only eight miles. I could give you a lift on my scooter —" he said.

"Oh! Do you live in Glendarroch?"

"No, I live in Auchtarne, but —"

"But that would be taking you miles out of your way. I couldn't possibly —"

"That's nothing," said Hector boldly, the woman's apparent helplessness bringing out the most masculine in him. "Just wait till I get the scooter started and we'll be off. Have you any luggage?"

"Only my handbag. I've just been to my sister's in Glasgow for the day, you see."

A little later the engine putt-putted into life and he climbed on to the saddle.

"I'm afraid you'll have to put your arms round me to be safe," he said a little shyly.

"Oh, that's all right. I feel quite safe with you," she said.

He detected a quick flash of knees and thigh as she put a leg

over the scooter and sat on the rear end of the saddle, and he felt
an unaccustomed stirring in his loins. He was aware of a bare
knee on either side of him, the skirt riding high as the legs
splayed out to accommodate the scooter, and a moment later
he shivered as a pair of arms crept round his waist and clasped
him firmly. This close physical contact was something he had
never experienced before.

He gulped and started with something of a jerk.

"Sorry," he said as he felt the arms tighten round his waist.

"It's quite all right."

A few minutes later they left the lights of Auchtarne behind
them and the scooter's little headlight cut a thin swathe through
the darkness of the country road which wound between the
trees towards Auchtarne.

She chattered as he propelled the scooter through the night.
She was the minister's housekeeper, she told him, just
appointed a month or so ago, and she had been to Glasgow to
arrange with her two sisters to come to Glendarroch the
following week to attend her birthday party which the minister
was allowing her to have in the manse. It was all very exciting
and wasn't it generous of the minister and she was looking
forward to it and her name was Lizzie Crossan and what was
his?

He told her, shouting back over his shoulder, and the journey
to Glendarroch had never seemed shorter. When he drew the
scooter to a halt outside the front door of the manse she hopped
off so quickly that he hadn't time to see much of her knees and
thighs and then he found himself being kissed on the cheek.

"Thank you so much, Mr Mack. Will you come to my
birthday party too?"

"Oh, I don't think —"

"Thursday next week at seven o'clock. Do come."

Mr Purdie would be back next week, and he switched to early
shift, so there was nothing to stop him.

"Well, thank you, I'd like to," he said.

He rode back to Auchtarne feeling strangely lightheaded,
and as he pushed the scooter on to its rack at the side of the
bungalow where he lived with his mother, he wondered

whether it was wise to move out into the unknown world like this. What would his mother think? He hoped that she was asleep and that he could get into the house without waking her and causing her to wonder why he was so late in getting home.

The following Thursday he lied to his mother for the first time in his life. He told her he was going to the pictures. Fortunately she didn't ask why he was wearing his best suit for that, and he left on the scooter and drove to the manse in Glendarroch.

It was a very pleasant party. Lizzie had made a punch with a couple of bottles of wine, but he didn't take any of that because the weather was particularly warm, even for August, so he stuck to lemonade. He also knew he would have to ride back to Auchtarne afterwards. He met several people, including the minister who made him very welcome, and there were also Lizzie's sisters from Glasgow. There was a bright, rather too pretty one called Florence, and there was a much more solid and dependable-looking one called Mary. Something seemed to draw him to Mary throughout the evening. Perhaps it was her concern for her sister Lizzie. Lizzie had told her that he had given her a lift to Glendarroch the previous week, and Mary had obviously been full of suspicion to begin with. A most commendable attitude, he thought, since neither of them knew him. But as the evening had progressed she had clearly become aware that he had intended Lizzie no harm, and they began to converse on a number of matters of interest to them both. The fact that they were both drinking the same thing helped to establish a rapport between them. She told him a lot about her church in Glasgow and the shortcomings of the minister there, and in turn he was able to tell her about the church he attended in Auchtarne, and he voiced a few doubts about his own minister's doctrine. They both agreed that neither of them had been to the church in Glendarroch and it would be interesting to hear Mr MacPherson preach. Mary Crossan told him that he had recently lost his wife which she felt would probably give his sermons a depth of feeling unobtainable in most other churches.

He left early, partly because he would have to be up at six-thirty for his shift and partly because the pictures in Auchtarne finished at ten o'clock and if he wasn't back shortly after that his mother would wonder where he was, and he drove through the bright evening humming snatches of popular songs. What an odd thing to do. But his whole world seemed suddenly to have opened out into vast new and inexplicable vistas.

Next day he saw Mary and Florence Crossan at the station on their way back to Glasgow. They didn't speak, because of course they had return tickets, but he managed to attract their attention from the ticket-room door, waving to them.

Florence waved cheerfully back, but it was Mary he watched more carefully. She saw him and inclined her head in acknowledgement just as the train drew to a halt at the platform, and that inclination of the head meant a lot more to him than Florence's cheerful wave.

The guard's whistle blew, the driver responded with a whistle from the engine. Steam billowed along the platform and the train began to move out. The steam obscured the carriage window for a moment, and then miraculously cleared so that he had a last picture of Mary sitting in the window seat facing him. She seemed to be looking at him as the train drew away. He hoped so.

Things had returned to normal, he felt, as he closed the ticket office door. Just as they had been a week or so ago. But if that were the case, why was it that he felt so much more empty now than he had then?

16

Brian threw the shaws on the compost heap and dropped the potatoes into the wooden box at his feet.

"There you are," he said. "That should keep you going over the weekend."

From his kitchen chair at the back door Malcolm nodded expressionlessly.

"Come on, young James, let's take these in to Gran, shall we?" said Brian, unstrapping his son from the pram and lifting

him out. "Time you were indoors, Dad," he said to his father.
"It's getting chilly."

Malcolm nodded again and Brian watched sadly as he got to
his feet and began to stumble painfully towards the back door.
He followed with Jimmy in one arm and the potato box in the
other hand.

His mother was preparing the tea when he went in and he
handed Jimmy to her while he washed his hands at the sink. He
caught her eye as he did so and raised his own questioningly.
She shook her head, sadly, briefly in reply.

"How's Isabel?" she asked as Malcolm shuffled through to
the living-room, though that wasn't the subject they had been
silently discussing. It had been his father. He saw now with
hindsight that the reason why Malcolm had made over the store
and the post office to him was not because he had an
overwhelming desire to grow vegetables in his back garden. He
had never actually managed to do that. It had been because he
had known even at that time that there was something wrong,
that he wouldn't be able to continue himself and that the
change-over ought to be effected as soon as possible. Whether
he had realised it was Parkinson's disease or not, Brian didn't
know. Probably not.

"She's fine," he said.

"We haven't seen her for a while."

Brian glanced at the door through to the living-room and
lowered his voice.

"Well, she feels that you've got enough on your plate now
without having to think about her."

"Och now, that's nonsense. She's always welcome and you
tell her so. Besides, she wouldn't be a problem. She'd be a
help."

"I'll pack her along here, then. I'd better get young James
back or she'll be worrying that we've both been run over."

"All right, dear. See you soon."

"Of course."

He didn't like the anxious, slightly lost look in his mother's
eyes as he strapped Jimmy into his pram and pushed it down
the path to the gate. She stood watching them and waving until

the trees hid the view of the front door, and as he pushed the pram up the gentle slope towards the store he had a sudden vision of the transience of life: the new life in the pram where Jimmy was gurgling and experimenting with unformed speech, and his father, slowly but quietly sinking beside the fire at home. And there he was in the middle, like the ham in a ham sandwich, half way between the two.

He shivered and pushed the pram a little faster up the slope.

17

The letter came on the 1st December and he opened it with trembling fingers.

The relief was enormous. His application for a transfer had been approved. He was to start in the ticket office at St Enoch Station in Glasgow on 2nd January.

Hector was delighted. Everything seemed to have been devised by a divine providence and he wondered why he should have been singled out for such special attention.

He left the bungalow to start the back shift at Auchtarne station, closing the front door and locking it carefully as he had learnt to do since his mother's death six weeks before. That had been one of the reasons he had applied for the transfer, of course. He found he didn't want to stay on in the bungalow without her. A major root of his life had been torn out and he felt it was time to make the break complete.

But he wondered if there mightn't be a stronger reason for getting away.

Since that party at Glendarroch he had contrived to see Lizzie Crossan once or twice and had managed to get certain titbits of information out of her. It hadn't been difficult. Lizzie was a simple soul, innocent and unversed in the ways of the world, and a few questions had given him the answer he wanted: where Mary and Florence lived in Glasgow.

Now he could put the next phase of his cunning plan into operation. He would find himself lodgings somewhere close by and then, once the New Year came in, he would be within reach of Miss Crossan. He must remember that that was how he had to address her, although she had already become Mary in his mind.

He had thought of little else since that party and in a way she had grown in his mind into something bigger than he really liked to contemplate. This feeling had become stronger since his mother's death. His mother had looked after him, prepared his meals, made his bed, comforted him ever since he could remember. Through the fifty-seven years of his life she had always been there, and although he had known instinctively that by the laws of nature she would be gathered first, the event when it came had shocked him, leaving him shivering and naked in the cold. It was after that that he had found his thoughts turning more and more to that strong, dependable, capable woman he had met at Lizzie Crossan's birthday party.

Now, possibly, he had the chance of renewing that acquaintance. Perhaps, he thought with a thrill of fear, of developing it into something stronger.

18

Her father was at the door as the car drove in under the porch.

"Good to see you, my dear," he said as she climbed heavily and awkwardly out. "How are you?"

"Stiff, Dad, but otherwise fine."

"And you, Peter? What's this about only staying three days, eh?"

"I've got an appointment on the second which I can't get out of," said Peter, "and I don't like Elizabeth being too far from the hospital."

"Quite right, my boy. Good thinking. And how is my grandson, eh?"

"Kicking very hard," said Elizabeth with feeling.

"Rugby player, is he? Glad to hear it. Need chaps with backbone these days. Leave the luggage, Peter. Menzies will bring it in."

She followed him into the hall where there was much activity preparing for the New Year Ball the following night. Peggy and John were setting the chairs in the alcove under the stairs for the band, and there was Archie Menzies up a ladder fixing a paper chain to the cornice.

"Hello, Archie," she said. "How's Mrs Archie?"

"Complaining as usual," he said indistinctly because he had a drawing pin clasped in his teeth. "It's her back this time. Good to see you home, Mrs Cunningham."

"Fetch the luggage will you, Menzies?" said Father.

"Right away, Sir Logan," said Archie, and he pinned the end of the paper chain to the cornice and stepped down the ladder.

"Someone I want you to meet, Elizabeth," said Father. "That is if you're not too tired."

"Not I."

"Your mother's pottering about somewhere," he said vaguely as he led the way to the back of the hall and through the green baize door to the servants' quarters. "God knows what she's up to. Not flower arranging. There aren't any in the garden after the gales we've been having and the damned things don't seem to grow in the conservatory."

He stopped at the door to the factor's office and opened it. Of course, thought Elizabeth, he wants me to meet the new factor, the man who starts officially on the first of January when Martin Mackinlay retires after thirty years with the estate.

"Strachan, I want you to meet my daughter. Elizabeth, my dear, Paul Strachan, our new factor."

Paul Strachan rose from behind the desk. He was a small dark man with small dark eyes half-hidden by rimless glasses and he had shiny dark hair. When he smiled he did so with his teeth and left his eyes dark. There was one adjective which she thought described him accurately. Oily.

"Mrs Cunningham, a great pleasure," he said. His voice was soft and there was a hiss to the sibilants which reminded her of a snake. She didn't usually react strongly to people's physical shortcomings on first meeting them, but she took an instant dislike to Paul Strachan.

As the man enquired after her journey and her health and her life in Edinburgh, she wondered whether she wasn't being unfair. Nothing that he said could have caused offence, either in word or tone. Anyone who replaced Martin Mackinlay was bound to start at a disadvantage, but she had been prepared to make allowances for that. Even so, the touch of his hand in hers made her flesh creep. It was damp and — oily. The word came again and she thought of Uriah Heep.

Later she tentatively asked her father about him. Where did he come from, why had he appointed a man like that? Sir Logan became defensively tetchy.

"Factors don't grow on trees these days, my dear," he said. "The man is efficient. That's what we want."

"You've checked his references?"

"I've done everything, since you weren't here to take your share of the responsibility," he said sharply. "After all, Strachan will last into your time, you know."

As she changed for dinner that night she felt disappointed. And she had been looking forward to the New Year Ball so much. Not that in her present state she could take much part in it physically, but she could be there, a part of the annual event which had become an integral part of the estate year. But now there was this man, this stranger. . . . She looked out towards the loch from the window. It was dark, of course, but there was a moon and the bare trees stood still and silent before the silver sheen of the loch. It was just the same. But things were changing, nevertheless. For the first time she felt that there was more than a sheet of window glass between the estate and herself.

19

The Bonaly Street Church Hall resembled the Bonaly Street Church: large, draughty, grey and dull. Hector Mack pushed open the door and entered, feeling little difference in the temperature inside from what he had felt outside where the pavements were covered in dirty snow and the wind seemed to whistle into your face round every corner.

He had attended the Bonaly Street Church two weeks ago

and when, last Sunday, the minister had announced from the pulpit that the monthly social evening would take place this Thursday he knew that he was about to reach the climax of his pursuit, and now he found his heart beating a little faster as he surveyed the slightly misty scene before him.

There were perhaps a dozen women in assorted headgear scattered around the hall, evidently waiting for a tea urn to boil, and he peered shortsightedly at each of them in turn, feeling a growing sense of disappointment that none of them was Mary Crossan. However, he had no sooner made that unfortunate discovery than a door at the back of the hall opened and Mary herself came in followed by Mr Robertson, the minister, an elderly, desiccated, intensely grey person with a permanent drip on the end of his nose.

Mary caught sight of him immediately, frowned a little, said something to the minister and then came towards him.

"What are you doing here?" she demanded.

It wasn't quite what he had expected. Perhaps over the weeks he had built up impossibly romantic notions of how their first meeting might be. And was there a slight disappointment in meeting her again? Had he built up a picture in his mind over the past weeks of someone younger, finer, more — more attractive? Surely not. . . .

"Good evening, Miss Crossan," he said. "I — I heard about the social evening in church last Sunday, so I —"

"You were in church on Sunday?"

"I have attended divine service here every Sunday since I arrived in Glasgow at the end of December," he said.

Her attitude softened slightly.

"I haven't seen you in church," she said, and he was about to explain that each Sunday this month he had been on the early shift so that it had been the evening service he had attended so far, but she didn't give him a chance. "The urn is not yet boiling," she said and he blinked at the change of subject and forgot what he had been about to say.

"That's all right," he said. "I had my tea at my lodgings before I came out."

"You have lodgings near here?"

"Yes. Funny, isn't it? Just round the corner, in fact. I — er — I hadn't realised you lived so close."

Lizzie Crossan had told him that her sisters lived at Queen's Park, but when he had found out the name of the street from her a crafty study of the Glasgow street map had shown him that it wasn't quite Queen's Park. Really it was closer to Govanhill, but Lizzie was a useful informant. From what she said he had managed to find lodgings within easy reach of the church which the Crossans attended.

She seemed to approve of what he told her, and she took him to a chair and made him sit down and brought the minister over and introduced him, though he had of course already met Mr Robertson when he had first attended the Bonaly Street Church, and a little later she brought a cup of tea for each of them from the successfully boiled urn, and he felt a familiar sense of comfort and belonging slip over him again. It was as though his mother were looking after him once more. And as he watched Mary moving capably around getting the gramophone ready for the Scottish country dancing they were about to indulge in, he realised that there was a very comforting physical resemblance as well.

20

She was very tired. And very contented. And really it hadn't taken so long as it might have done and it hadn't been as painful as she had been led to believe it usually was.

She lay nestled into the pillows, warm and comfortable. Outside the windows of the Simpson Memorial Maternity Pavilion other buildings of the Royal Infirmary of Edinburgh were grey and dull in the January light. She looked down at the red, wrinkled face of her daughter with a mixture of awe and pride. So small, so perfect, so helpless to be brought into this big, wide, uncaring world, she thought.

"It's the same for all of us, Mrs Cunningham," said the matter-of-fact voice of the sister, and she realised that she must have spoken aloud. "Your husband's here. Would you like to see him now?"

She nodded and a few moments later Peter bent over her and kissed her and she responded weakly and happily.

"Isn't she beautiful?" she asked.

He nodded and ran a finger gently round the baby's chin. The screwed-up eyes opened momentarily, didn't like what they saw and closed again as she gave an enormous yawn.

"You're a clever girl," said Peter.

"Her or me?" asked Elizabeth.

"Both of you. And yes, she is beautiful. Takes after her mother, fortunately."

"Are you pleased about her?"

"Delighted."

"Dad won't be. He wanted a grandson."

"You're not thinking of putting her back, are you?"

"Certainly not. I don't think she'd fit any more. Dad'll just have to wait."

"Better luck next time," said Peter with a chuckle. "You're sure about the name?"

She nodded.

"Are you?" she asked.

"Positive. I'll register her tomorrow." He looked down at his daughter again. "Welcome to the world, Fiona Cunningham," he said.

21

Brian came into the living-room and shut the door very quietly.

"Isabel's with her," he said.

David nodded and Brian crossed to the chair on the other side of the fire and sat down. David held out the whisky bottle but Brian shook his head and there was silence for a long time while the bleak February wind howled round the window and tried to get in.

It was the first time they had been alone, thought Brian, and now there really wasn't anything to say.

"I'd no idea it was so bad," said David at last.

"He went very quickly towards the end," said Brian.

"Probably just as well. No one wanted to see him suffer. There wasn't any pain. Just helplessness. You know how he must have hated that."

David nodded and the silence descended again. A coal falling in the grate was startling and, more to break the silence than anything else, Brian leant forward and poked the fire, sending a shower of sparks flying up the chimney. The flames danced on the wall, giving the illusion of warmth, but it was bitterly cold. It had been very difficult breaking open the grave for the funeral that morning. The ground was frozen rock solid.

"I was hoping he'd meet Helen," said David.

"Helen?"

"Yes. I'll bring her up in the summer some time. When things have settled a bit. When Mum's back to normal. That sort of thing."

"Is it serious?"

David nodded, staring into the fire.

"Oh, yes," he said.

"Good. I'm glad," said Brian. "And Mum will be too. Maybe you should tell her before you go back."

"I'll see how the land lies."

The silence fell again.

Isabel came quietly into the room.

"She's asleep," she said.

She came and sat down beside Brian and he put an arm round her shoulder, drawing comfort from her presence. He looked at his brother, sitting opposite. David was crouched forward towards the fire, his hands held out to it. The red light lit his face, lost and puzzled. David was the clever one, he thought, the one who got the high marks at school, the one who went to university and for whom the world was an oyster. Yet in these circumstances his cleverness meant nothing, his degree from Aberdeen was an empty symbol. They had never had much in common, really, but now he felt that for the first time they had. It was tragic that it had to be the death of their father which had brought them together at last.

22

Jimmy Shand and his band burst into the *Gay Gordons* and Hector Mack and Mary Crossan retired to two wooden chairs at the side of the hall. He had discovered over the last two months that Mary wouldn't do the *Gay Gordons*, considering it undignified, a sentiment with which he found himself in hearty agreement. It was also physically exhausting. They watched the gyrating and promenading couples for a few minutes, and then he deliberately unclenched his fists.

"Miss Crossan," he said and gulped nervously.

"Yes, Mr Mack," she said.

"I have sold my mother's bungalow in Auchtarne."

"How interesting."

"I am in the process of purchasing a small property in Pollokshaws with the proceeds."

"An extremely residential district."

"Isn't it? The bungalow is very similar to my mother's. It has three rooms, kitchen and bathroom —"

"And do you intend to occupy this bungalow yourself, Mr Mack, or are you thinking of sharing it with some other suitable person in railway employment?"

"No —"

"It sounds a large place for a single gentleman."

"Yes. Yes, it is. Far too big for me alone. Miss Crossan —"

"Yes?"

"I find myself in a quandary, not quite knowing how to proceed. You and your sisters are orphans, you see."

"Yes, Mr Mack, I am aware of that. What has it do do with a bungalow in Pollokshaws?"

"A great deal, actually. And you are the oldest sister."

"That is true, but not by very much."

"But that is what makes my position so awkward, you see."

"You wish to change your seat? I quite understand. We *are* rather close to the dance here."

"No, no! It's not that position. You see, I do not know who I should approach for permission to pay my respects to you."

"Your respects, Mr Mack? I have always regarded you as an extremely respectful person. I may also say an extremely respectable person."

"To pay my respects with a view to possible matrimony," he said desperately, and hoped that he hadn't raised his voice sufficiently for anyone else to hear. However, it seemed that the physical exertion of the *Gay Gordons* and the volume of Jimmy Shand and his band had successfully allowed him to maintain his secret.

She turned and stared at him and he found it difficult to meet her eye. He looked guiltily away and studied two large ladies gyrating in front of him, and wondered which of them was dancing the male part.

"I *am* over twenty-one, Mr Mack."

"Naturally . . . I mean, one wouldn't have thought so, but you must be. I mean —"

"Therefore there is no need for anyone else to be consulted."

He looked at her with a mixture of hope and trepidation.

"You mean — you mean, you would yourself consider a proposal of marriage?"

She thought about it for a moment while he held his breath and the dance throbbed on.

"I can see no reason why not," she said.

He gulped again and took a very deep breath.

"Then will you marry me, Miss Crossan?"

"Thank you, Mr Mack. I should be very pleased," she said.

23

"Fiona, I baptise you in the name of the Father, and of the Son, and of the Holy Spirit. Amen. The blessing of God Almighty, Father, Son, and Holy Spirit, descend upon you, and dwell in your heart for ever. Amen."

Then the organ pealed and the congregation behind and on both sides of them burst into that part of the service of baptism which always brought tears to Elizabeth's eyes.

The Lord bless you and keep you: the Lord make his face to shine upon you, and be gracious unto you, the Lord lift up his countenance upon you, and give you peace.

Old quavery voices, young crystal-clear voices, strong male voices and pure female voices, the whole estate combined into that one beautiful wish echoing up into the roof of the church, spreading and then pouring down a blessing on her daughter who lay in Mr MacPherson's practised arms, a slight frown on her face as she thought about that little cross of water on her forehead, perhaps listening to the glorious, resonant light around her, and Elizabeth found her eyes stinging with happiness and a sense of humility.

Later she stood with Fiona in her arms outside the church, making sure that her shadow stayed between the little face and the strong April sun, while the people came to admire her and wish her well, and her parents stood proudly beside her, basking in this very special occasion, and she was aware of Peter waiting impatiently some distance away, worried that his daughter might catch cold, she supposed, though really it wasn't all that cold and Fiona was well wrapped up against the chill of an April morning.

At last she could get away and she joined Peter at the car and climbed in while he came round to the driver's side and slammed the car door shut with unaccustomed violence.

"What's the matter?" she asked in surprise.

He didn't say anything until he'd started the engine and the car moved away down the road towards the Big House.

"What is it, Peter?" she asked.

His knuckles were tense and white on the wheel.

"You're going to have to tell your father that our daughter is not going to become a chattel of the Glendarroch estate," he said.

"What do you mean?"

"Everyone treats her as if she belonged to *them*. Not to *us*," he said, swinging the car round a corner so that she had to put out a hand to prevent herself from being knocked against the door pillar.

"Of course she belongs to us," she protested. "I don't think anyone was saying otherwise."

"Fiona is not going to be taken over by Glendarroch," he said.

She felt a stirring of anger in her.

"You mean she's going to belong exclusively to the legal fraternity in Edinburgh?" she said.

"That's ridiculous."

"It's what you're saying."

"It's nothing of the sort. I just don't want my daughter brought up to become a part of this feudal rigmarole of landed gentry and tenants —"

"Peter, you're jealous."

She tried to laugh off his anger, but it was the wrong thing to do.

"Oh, that's right. Laugh," he said. "That's the answer to everything, isn't it? Laugh at it. Your father wanted a grandson so that the succession was safe, didn't he? He's still hoping for that, but if he doesn't get it then Fiona will be good enough. So long as the succession is assured. My God, she's got to be saved from that sort of fate —"

"Now, wait a minute," she said, and she could feel the blood pounding in her veins. She made a determined effort to control herself, to keep calm and cool. It would be wrong to indulge in a major quarrel on a day like this, of all days, the day when their daughter was christened, the day which should be one of the highlights in both their lives.

"I think it's maybe a bit early to start deciding what Fiona's going to do with her life, don't you? Probably she'll end up wanting to be a vet or a nurse. By the time she gets to the right age they might even have female engine drivers. You never know."

Fiona opened her eyes and began to cry for the first time since they had left the house for the Sunday service, and Elizabeth seized on the noise with relief.

"No, all right. Sorry. She doesn't like that idea," she said. "Leave out the engine driving bit."

Peter grunted and she saw the knuckles relax on the wheel

and she sat back with a silent sigh of relief. The danger was past.
For the time being.

24

The damp and chill of winter lingered into May in the Bonaly
Street Church, and Mr Robertson had a cold, whether a
summer or a winter one, he seemed unable to decide. The
attempt to brighten the pulpit with a bunch of tulips had failed
dismally and the tulips drooped as though they too had been
affected by the lingering winter.

Mr Robertson's voice was hoarse and his nose bore an even
longer drip than usual as he conducted the wedding service. No
matter how often he wiped it on a large and none-too-clean
handkerchief the drip persisted in reappearing. Hector found it
difficult to keep his eyes off it and concentrate on what the
minister was saying. In spite of the hoarseness his voice echoed
round the huge, gloomy building, accentuating the smallness of
the congregation, which consisted of Lizzie Crossan, who
seemed to think she was watching some dreadful comic turn in
a music hall, because she seemed unable to restrain her giggles,
and Florence, who was trying to keep her sister quiet but
evidently wasn't taking the ceremony very seriously either.
Apart from them there was no one in the pews save for a couple
of vagrants who found the church more comforting than the
thin drizzle of rain outside, and the beadle who seemed to be
impatient to lock up. And there was, of course, Mr Mack's
immediate superior in the ticket office at St Enoch who had
volunteered to act as his best man since there was no one else to
do the job. Mr Watson was a large, jovial man with a very red
face who, rumour had it, indulged in strong drink on Saturday
nights and was often heard singing in the bath around
midnight. Even he seemed affected by the atmosphere today,
for he didn't look in the least like singing at the moment.
Perhaps he had undertaken the duty in the belief that after the
ceremony there would be strong drink.

Mr Robertson, clearly keen to get back to his manse and his

bed, hurried through the ceremony at top speed, barely giving them time to make their vows, then rushed them into the vestry and had them sign the register and on their way out before they could draw breath.

They walked down the silent aisle to the door, unaccompanied by joyful music. Hector had asked the organist to come and play at the ceremony, but it was a Saturday afternoon and the organist had managed to get a ticket for the cup final.

Lizzie and Florence joined them at the porch where they stood sheltering from the rain until a passing taxi answered their frantic waves. Hector helped his bride into it and said importantly to the driver, "Central Station, please", and then sat back with a sigh as they began their journey to the week's honeymoon which he had booked at a boarding house in Rothesay. It was a silent journey. The new Mrs Mack seemed little inclined to conversation, and he felt the same himself. Somehow it had all happened without his volition. It had been inevitable and preordained and, as throughout his life, he had simply allowed himself to be whirled along by the tide, letting it take him where it wished. Now here he was, fifty-eight years old and for the first time in his life a married man with a married man's responsibilities. He shivered slightly. Probably the after-effects of the atmosphere in the Bonaly Street Church.

Of course it was all right, he told himself dubiously. Of course it was. Naturally he hadn't made a mistake . . . Had he?

Chapter Two
1963-65
1

Perhaps New Years made you look at things with new eyes, thought Sir Logan as he came through the green baize door into the hall again.

He had just been to the kitchen to make his speech to the staff, welcoming the New Year of 1963. They had all been there, Syme, Mrs Syme, Menzies, Mrs Archie, Peggy and John. As usual he'd thanked them for their work in the past, looked forward to the future with the usual optimism, had been given a glass of whisky and drunk their health, and now he was about to make his other-side-of-the-door speech.

Things changed. That was inevitable, he supposed, but this year saw a bigger change than usual. The retirement of Martin Mackinlay meant that they now no longer had a band formed from people on the estate. Mackinlay had been a champion fiddler in his day and even the year he retired his fingers had still been remarkably nimble on the strings. But that was two years ago. Last year they'd tried to make do without him and it had been a disaster, so this year they'd had to hire a band from Auchtarne for the occasion. Not the same thing at all, he thought, as he listened to the waltz they were playing. He had no ear for music, of course, but the racket sounded thinner to him than it had done in past years.

He moved round the guests sitting and standing around the edge of the hall. There seemed fewer of them than before. Dammit, he remembered in his young day when you couldn't move in the hall for people. Like the damned Black Hole of Calcutta. Now — he made a rough count. Twenty people? Not many more.

He stopped in a corner by himself, curiously unwilling to socialise for a moment, and watched Elizabeth and Peter dancing the waltz together. Their faces were set, they said nothing and Sir Logan frowned. All was not well there, he thought. He wasn't an unduly sensitive man, he knew that, but, dammit, he knew an atmosphere when he came across one. All marriages had their ups and downs, of course. They'd had them themselves, he and Dorothy. Be damned boring if you didn't. He hoped this was only a temporary down, if only for the sake of that little scrap sleeping upstairs. He smiled to himself. He had to admit he'd grown extraordinarily fond of the little mite, so small, yet holding such a large slice of his heart. Not so small now, either. Gad, she'd be two in three weeks' time. Nothing like grandchildren to make you realise how damned quickly time passed.

And there was the man Strachan dancing with Lady Strathmorris while old Strathmorris was, he presumed, propping up the bar in the morning-room as usual. Cynthia didn't look as if she was enjoying herself much, but then Cynthia never did. Always worrying whether Arthur was going to make a damned fool of himself again. Strachan was talking to her, his face fixed in a friendly yet respectful smile, exactly right for the status of his partner. Elizabeth had spoken to him about the man again today, and he had to admit he was beginning to have doubts about him himself. Nothing he could put a finger on. Just his manner. He did his job quietly and efficiently, keeping the boring details away from him, but he was beginning to wonder whether he mightn't have been precipitate offering the man a fifteen-year contract. Dammit, he'd still got thirteen years to go from tonight. . . .

"Time for your speech, Logan," said Dorothy.

He hadn't heard her approach, he'd been so busy with these disturbing and uncomfortable thoughts.

"At the end of this dance, my dear. Then you and I will have to take the floor together again, old girl, eh?"

"Of course."

He squeezed her hand with unaccustomed affection. She was wearing a pale blue ball gown sort of thing with the rope of pearls he'd given her on their tenth anniversary.

"You look ravishing, my dear," he said.

She smiled at him, a grateful, slightly sad smile.

"You were always an expert flatterer, Logan," she said.

"No flattery about it, Dorothy. Mean every word of it —"

He stopped and coughed in sudden embarrassment. Damn silly romantic sort of conversation for two people of their age, he thought, but as he looked at her he felt a wealth of sadness and nostalgia sweep over him. She actually looked tired, under the magnificent dress and the jewellery and the make-up. Tired and old. Just as he felt himself.

The band finished uncertainly but more or less at the same time and he made sure his sporran and tie were straight before stepping out on to the floor to make his speech welcoming 1963.

2

"Do you think he's lonely?"

Brian looked at his son who was staggering along the path ahead of them. The sun was bright today and the leaves were beginning to burst from their buds. The water of the loch lay blue and calm. It was a perfect April Sunday afternoon. He clasped Isabel's hand and squeezed it.

"He's not lonely," he said. "He's got us."

"I know. But later . . ."

"Later he'll have thousands of friends at school."

"Thousands?"

"Well, ten or twenty, maybe. That should be enough for most people."

"Yes, I know, but —"

"Isabel, stop worrying."

He swung her round to face him and put his hands on her shoulders. She *was* worrying, he could see. She had been worrying for a long time. And so, he had to admit, was he.

"There's plenty of time," he said.

Jimmy had found something interesting to examine on the shore of the loch and they watched as he crouched down and picked up a round stone which seemed to sparkle in the sunlight. He came trotting back to them with it and handed it to Brian.

"Precuss," he said.

Brian took it.

"Probably a diamond," he said. "See if you can find some more, eh?"

Jimmy nodded and trotted unsteadily back to the shore and the line of pebbles which fringed it. He began to search with great diligence and seriousness.

They sat down on a fallen log and he put an arm round her.

"I wonder if I should see Dr Wallace," she said

"It might be a good idea if you're going to go on worrying yourself into a nervous breakdown about it."

"On the other hand —"

She broke off and he felt her shiver.

"On the other hand what?"

"Well — maybe it isn't meant that we should have another child."

"Good Lord, that sounds terribly old fashioned and presbyterian."

"No, I mean it, Brian. Maybe God or nature or whatever you like to call it is telling us to stop trying."

"Stop trying? Woman what are you saying? Are you tired of me, or something?"

"No. Oh, no. How could I be? It's just that — Och, I don't know. I'm blethering. Come on. It's getting chilly and I've got the tea to get."

She stood up suddenly and began to walk slowly back towards the village, hands in her pockets, head down. He called to Jimmy who came reluctantly with a pebble in each hand which he passed solemnly to Brian who put them equally solemnly in his coat pocket.

He walked thoughtfully with Jimmy who was chattering inconsequentially beside him and he only had to say "Yes" or "No" at the right time, while his mind was on other things.

Maybe Isabel was right. Maybe it wasn't meant that they should have another child. Certainly the lack of a brother or sister for Jimmy wasn't for want of trying, but it was more than three years since Jimmy was born and there was no sign of Isabel getting pregnant again.

He supposed it wasn't all that important. They already had a son. That was more than many people were able to have and perhaps they should be thankful. But Isabel was worrying and that worry was going to grow if there was still no sign of a child as time continued to pass by.

3

The still, warm air was filled with the bleating of sheep. Donald Lachlan forced the last of them through the dip and watched as it emerged, staggering and shaking itself, into the freedom of the field at the other end.

He was a small, wiry man with crinkly red hair and a face lined and seamed with the weather on the hill.

"That's it, then, Jamie," he said, turning and leaning on the fence of the pen where the undipped sheep had been held and which was now empty.

"Aye." Jamie Stewart joined him and Donald offered him his tobacco pouch. Jamie took it, filled his pipe and they lit up, leaning contentedly against the pen, the rich smell of the tobacco floating into the air above them, the sky blue and flecked with pure white clouds. It was the contentment which came at the end of a hard spell of work.

Jamie spat suddenly.

"That man Strachan," he said, and left it at that.

"Aye. Him," said Donald.

There didn't seem to be much else to say. The tone of their voices had told each other what they thought of the man.

"He's over there, you ken," said Jamie with a very small nod in the direction of a clump of trees at the far side of the field.

"Aye. Skulking," Donald agreed.

"What do you think he's up to, eh?"

"Making notes. He's aye making notes, that man."

"Mphm. Probably about another rent rise."

It was Donald's turn to spit, which he did with much feeling.

"I wouldn't wonder," he said. "Mind Old Mackinlay?"

"Now there was a man."

"Aye. A pity he's gone. If he ever came up hereabouts at least he'd drop in for a cup of tea and a chat, tell you the news of the village. Ask how the bairns were. You get nothing like that from this one."

"That's right. A scunner, that's what he is."

There was a shout behind them and they turned, watching the two youngsters racing up the slope towards them. Morag was first as usual, outstripping Dougal and gaining as she came.

Jamie chuckled appreciatively.

"That's the school bus in for the last time," he said. "She's got a fair turn of speed in her," he said.

"She has that," Donald agreed, "but has she the staying power?"

"Staying power? Man, she could be up Ben Darroch and down again without getting breathless —"

Morag arrived, flushed and laughing, and a moment later Dougal reached them too.

"Well?" said Donald as his son joined them. "Where's the schoolbag, then?"

"In the burn behind the High School," said Dougal joyfully. "Finished!"

He leapt in the air with a whoop of delight and Morag joined him.

"Book learning's been a waste of time on these two," said Donald. "Now the pair of you'll have to start learning about living."

"Tomorrow, Dad? Out on the hill?" asked Dougal eagerly.

"Tomorrow. Out on the hill," said Donald with a grin which faded as he turned and his eye caught that distant clump of trees. "And to hell with the man Strachan," he added.

4

The noise came again as he dragged himself out of sleep and for a while his muzzy mind refused to focus on it. Then he became aware of the fact that the other side of the bed was unoccupied and he came fully awake.

"Isabel?" he said.

There was silence for a moment and then her voice came from some distance away.

"Go back to sleep," she said.

"What time is it?"

"Not six o'clock yet."

He grunted and opened one eye. The summer light was shining through the curtains and as he registered it he heard the bathroom door close quietly.

That same noise came again, but more muffled this time, and now he knew what it was.

He sprang out of bed and hurried to the door, tripping over the suitcase which lay already packed.

"Isabel?"

He stopped outside the bathroom door. He heard her groan, a brief, muffled sound, cut off almost at source.

"Go back to bed," she said.

"What's wrong?"

"Nothing."

But immediately after she said it he heard it again.

"You're being sick . . ." he said.

He opened the door and found her bent over the lavatory pan, her face pale. She turned to him, wiping her mouth with a facecloth.

"It must have been something I ate," she said.

He looked searchingly at her and she avoided his eye.

"Tell me," he said, a terrible hope in his voice.

She sighed and turned away and picked up Jimmy's potty, carrying it back to the bedroom. She lay down on the bed.

"I — I don't dare to hope," she said. "This is the first time I've been sick. But I'm — I'm late . . ."

"I'll ring Wallace," he said.

"For goodness sake, don't be silly! Leave it till breakfast time at least."

He lay down beside her, propping himself on one elbow as he looked down at her, that wild hope beginning to beat in him.

"Do you really think —?" he asked.

"I don't know. But it looks like it," she said.

"Then that's it. We're not going to London. We're staying right here."

"Brian, don't be daft!"

"Daft? After all this time? Risk taking you to London? Nothing doing!"

"All right, maybe *I* shouldn't go. The way I feel at the moment I don't think I want to. But *you've* got to go —"

"No."

"It's your own brother's wedding."

"Then he'll have to do without me."

"There's nothing you can do staying here except get in the way and worry me."

"Listen, if you're pregnant I'm not going to leave you for a single minute . . ."

"You'll do what you're told."

"Who's the boss in this house?"

"I am, till you come to your senses again. Now look at what you've done," she went on as Jimmy began to cry in the next room. "You've woken him up."

"*I've* woken him up —?"

"Well, all right, *we've* woken him up. Now, I've got it all worked out. You will go and get Jimmy up and dressed and bring him through here. Then I'll allow you to go and make us some breakfast and when you've done that you can ring Dr Wallace. You have my full permission to do all that on one condition. And that is, after you've done it, you get on the bus and go to Auchtarne and catch the train to Glasgow and get to London and be at your brother's wedding and apologise for me not being there and then come home again."

"That's *one* condition?"

"Well, maybe it's got a few sub-clauses."

"I don't like it."

She put up her arms and pulled him down to her.

"You're lying," she said. "You love it. You love the whole glorious business."

5

"I'll take a packet of pandrops, please, Isabel," said Maggie, thumping a shilling on to the counter. "Brian off to David's wedding, then?"

Isabel gave her the pandrops and put the shilling in the till, handing over the change.

"Yes," she said.

"How long is he away for?"

"A week."

"So you're running the shop on your own?"

"Yes. I'm quite enjoying it, too."

"Funny things, men," observed Maggie.

"Do you mean funny ha-ha or funny-peculiar?"

"Oh, funny-peculiar, of course. I mean, fancy Brian going off to London and leaving you behind. Selfish, I call it."

"I made him go on his own."

"Why?"

"I just didn't feel like going."

That was a lie, thought Maggie. There was something evasive about Isabel and she wondered what it was.

"Seems odd to me," she said. "Still, maybe you don't see it that way."

"No, I don't."

"But about men. What I really mean is, look at my father. Then there's that Sorry Watson. He keeps sending me postcards of Lerwick. Awful bleak looking, Isabel."

"He's not coming back then?"

"Doesn't look like it. He was going to sell that smallholding but I don't expect he's finding it easy. Who'd want to buy a smallholding in Shetland, for goodness sake? Well, I'd better be off, I suppose . . ."

"Would you like a cup of tea?"

"Wouldn't I just," said Maggie, returning rapidly to the counter.

"The kettle's just boiling, I think. I usually have one about now. Won't be a moment."

Isabel turned to go through to the house and then suddenly stopped and bent over.

"What's wrong?" asked Maggie.

It was a moment before Isabel replied.

"Nothing," she said. "Just a paper clip. See?"

She held up her hand but Maggie couldn't see anything in it and Isabel hurried out before she could ask. Funny that. It was almost as if she'd had a sudden pain. . . . Maggie looked over the magazines on the table and then the shelves stacked with goods of all sorts. There was something comforting about the shop. Something permanent. You could buy anything here from a pie to a pot of paint. It was a good place to spend a few spare minutes. It was a good place to be when you had to get out of the house and away from that gasping, wheezing old man. Maybe she should do it more often, especially if Isabel started dispensing cups of tea. That would always be welcome between bus runs.

Yes, perhaps she'd make a point of dropping into the shop more often in future.

6

The London train had been late, so there had been no time to ring Isabel before the dash across Glasgow to Queen Street to catch the connection to Auchtarne. Now, as this train drew into Auchtarne, itself half an hour late, he was debating whether to ring from the station or simply get on to Maggie's bus and wait till he reached Glendarroch

In the end the decision was taken out of his hands. As he stepped off the train he found his mother waiting for him and the sight of her told him immediately that something must be very badly wrong.

"Isabel?" he asked.

"Brian, I'm sorry. She's in the cottage hospital," said Sandra.

He stared at her unbelievingly.

"What happened?"

"I'm not sure. All I know is that Jean found her this morning when she went to help her open the shop. She was in awful pain and she rang Dr Wallace."

They hurried out of the station and turned left at the end of the station yard to get to the hospital, his mother's steps reflecting his own urgency.

"They sent an ambulance and — and I think she may have lost the baby. I'm so sorry, Brian."

He said nothing. There was nothing to say. All those years of waiting, the sudden wild hope and then to have that hope crushed almost before it had been born. . . . He shouldn't have gone. His first instinct had been right, but she had made him go. . . .

It was beginning to get dark when they reached the hospital. The sun had set and the afterglow was beginning to fade from the sky.

Young Wallace was waiting for them.

"Brian, I'm glad you're here —" he began.

"Isabel —?" he asked

"She's all right."

"Can I see her?"

"No. Not tonight. Maybe tomorrow. She's not fully out of the anaesthetic yet."

Anaesthetic. . . . That sounded bad, too.

"What happened?"

"It was an ectopic pregnancy, Brian."

"Don't blind me with science. Just tell me what happened!"

"An ectopic pregnancy means that the child was beginning to form in the fallopian tube instead of in the womb. Isabel had been having bouts of pain for a day or two, but she'd said nothing about them, evidently. Then this morning it was so bad that she collapsed. We whipped her in here and I'm afraid we've had to terminate the pregnancy."

There it was, what he had been dreading from the moment he had seen his mother at the station.

"She's all right?"

"Yes . . ."

But there was reserve in Wallace's voice and he gripped his arm.

"What is it?"

"We had no alternative, Brian. We had to perform a hysterectomy."

"A hysterectomy . . . that means . . ."

"That means removing the womb and everything. I'm sorry. There can be no more children."

He sat down in a chair in the waiting-room while Wallace explained quietly what had happened, but he was no longer listening. He knew all that he had to know.

By the time Wallace had stopped talking the daylight had faded completely. Silence fell in the otherwise deserted waiting-room. After a moment, Wallace got up and went to switch on the light.

"Does she know?" Brian asked.

"Isabel? Yes . . ."

Again there was a slight note of reserve in his voice, but Brian was too overwhelmed to notice it.

"When can I see her?"

"Leave her tonight. First thing tomorrow she should be strong enough."

He and Sandra booked into the Auchtarne Arms. He asked about Jimmy, and Sandra told him that Jean was looking after him and he wasn't to worry about that. He spent a restless night in the strange bed, finding his thoughts revolving meaninglessly around in his head, and in the morning, sleepless and unrefreshed, he couldn't face breakfast. He bought a bunch of flowers as soon as the shops opened, and then went to the hospital.

It wasn't a normal visiting hour, but these weren't normal circumstances, and he was taken by a starched and antiseptic nurse to the side ward where Isabel was.

"Here you are now, Mrs Blair. Your husband's here to see you. Isn't that nice?" said the nurse with forced professional cheerfulness, and she left them together.

She lay against the pillows and she looked washed out. There was an intravenous drip in her arm. The life had gone from her face and he nearly cried out aloud at the look of her. She was pale and grey and her cheeks had sunk, but it was her eyes which riveted him and filled him with a nameless dread. They stared at him flatly, without emotion, without love and without kindness. He went to kiss her and she turned away from him.

He remembered the reserve in Wallace's voice and wondered whether this was the reason.

"Isabel —" he began, but she cut him off.

"Where were you?"

Her voice was low and hoarse from the anaesthetic and didn't sound like her at all.

"I didn't know —" he said.

"No, you didn't, did you? And you weren't there. There was no one there. You left me. You did this to me. It's all because of you."

"Isabel, I'm sorry —"

"That's not going to give me back to myself is it? I've lost it. I've lost *everything*."

He didn't know what to say and thought it better to say nothing. Her eyes closed and he wondered if she'd fallen asleep, but she hadn't. After a moment she turned her head away from him.

"Go away," she whispered, and when he hesitated she turned back to him, opened her eyes and stared at him with a look which he had never seen there before. "Go on. Get out!"

If she had had the strength she would have been shouting, he thought, and, confused and frightened by her attitude, he stepped backwards and left the side ward, still holding the flowers in his hand.

7

"No, no, no, Lizzie. Baked in the oven with a little milk, that's the proper way to do fish," said Mrs Mack.

"But Mr MacPherson likes his fish fried, Mary."

"Fried fish is very, very bad for him, as I shouldn't need to tell you."

"But — but there's no time to do it in the oven —"

"Then you should have started earlier. Come along now. I shall do it for you."

"But Mr MacPherson wants his tea at five o'clock. He has a choir practice —"

"You know what mother told us about fried fish, Lizzie?"

"I forgot."

"You forget too many things, my dear. You must try to remember."

"I do try, Mary, honestly I do, but —"

"Never mind. You just leave this to me."

She bustled about the kitchen, preparing the baked fish for the minister's tea while Lizzie hovered uncertainly in the background.

Mrs Mack looked round with disapproval. The kitchen was like a midden. Filthy dirty. The lunch dishes weren't even washed yet. By the Lord Harry, if she had Lizzie's job there would be changes here, she told herself.

But she had Hector to look after and that was her mission in life now, to make his life wholesome and clean and healthy, and though she regretted in many ways leaving him even for a day to the tender mercies of Florence in Glasgow to come and attend Lizzie's birthday party in the Glendarroch manse, she felt it was still her duty to act as a mother to Lizzie, who really wasn't terribly able to look after herself.

Hector was talking about perhaps coming to Auchtarne when he retired from the railways at the end of next year, and she had pooh-poohed the idea, telling him that he would miss the culture which was available to him in Glasgow and the company he had at the Bonaly Street Church.

Now, as she bustled about the kitchen of the manse, tidying up after Lizzie's futile messing about and preparing the minister's evening meal which would be a great deal more appetising and better for him than anything Lizzie would have prepared for him, she began to wonder whether Hector might not have a point. Not that she would agree to his retiring to Auchtarne, of course. But perhaps somewhere like Glendarroch where, she knew from what she had seen, there was

much effective work she could undertake, besides keeping an
eye on Lizzie at the manse.

8

Brian noticed that Dr Wallace had led him away from the shop
along the road in a direction where they could not be
overlooked from the bedroom window.

"What's happened to her?" he asked.

"It's not uncommon after a hysterectomy," said Wallace.

"But — but she's totally changed. I don't know what to do,"
said Brian in despair. "Is she ill? Is there anything I should do?"

"Yes, she's ill. But not physically. She's made a splendid
recovery from the operation. But sometimes the operation
itself does things to a woman's mind, especially a young woman
who has the right to expect to bear many more children."

"She rejects me."

Wallace nodded.

"It often happens this way. The woman blames what has
happened on the man who has caused it in the first place. You
have to understand that. It's unreasonable and ridiculous to the
normal person, but someone as young as Isabel who undergoes
a hysterectomy doesn't necessarily think normally."

"She was the sanest, most level-headed person I ever met,"
said Brian miserably.

"And they're often the ones who suffer most."

"Is there anything I can do?"

"Have patience. That's probably the toughest advice I can
give you, but it's very important. It's terribly trite to say that
time is the great healer, but in these circumstances it's true. Not
only that. It's probably the *only* healer."

He stopped and faced Brian.

"It's not going to be easy for you, Brian. In fact, it's going to
be damnably hard, but it's as well for you to know that so you
can be prepared for it. If there's anything I can do for you, any
help or advice I can give you, you only have to ask. And

remember you're not alone. Everyone's as concerned about Isabel as you are."

"How long will it take?"

"I don't know. Maybe a few weeks. Maybe a lot longer."

"How much longer?"

Wallace stared at him levelly for a moment.

"I can't predict that," he said gently.

Brian nodded dumbly, emptily, and watched as Wallace turned and walked towards his car, wondering what on earth he was going to do now that the whole purpose of his life — Isabel — seemed to have been cut off from him.

9

The clouds hung low over the loch, threatening snow, and Laird's Point was no place to bring a child on a morning like this. It was bitterly cold. Sir Logan took the small mittened hand in his own.

"Come on, little mouse," he said. "Back home, eh?"

Fiona obediently trotted along beside him, and he slowed his pace deliberately to accommodate hers. Their progress across the lawn towards the front door was marked by the tracks of his big boots and her small ones, side by side across the thick silver rime.

He sniffed the air, feeling good. It was one of his favourite times, this. The morning after the New Year Ball when the whole world was still asleep and he alone was awake, giving him a sense of superiority over his fellow human beings.

For the first time for many years he was sharing that feeling with someone else and he squeezed the hand in his affectionately, sharing the companionship.

"Dandad," said Fiona.

"Yes, my dear."

"See Mummy now?"

"I hope so, old girl."

"Mummy dessed now?"

"Bound to be. If she isn't we'll go and wake her, shall we?"

"Dess."

They went in through the front door and stood looking at the remains of last night's dance: the empty glasses on the tables, plates with half-eaten food . . .

"Messy," she announced.

"Quite right, my dear. Dreadful, isn't it?"

"Eddy messy," she confirmed and they crossed the hall to the staircase.

It had been a quieter ball again, he thought. And there had been no Peter. He hadn't been able to get away from Edinburgh, Elizabeth said. Well, he supposed a rising young lawyer did find it difficult to make spare time, and there was no doubt Peter was rising in the world, but at Hogmanay, dammit. . . . And Fiona was going to be three in three weeks' time. No sign of another one yet. He regretted that. Dammit, he loved this little mite, but she was only a girl, after all . . .

The green baize door at the back of the hall opened quietly just as they reached the turn of the stair and he peered over to see which of the staff was abroad so early. It wasn't yet nine o'clock.

Strachan.

"Good morning, Sir Logan," said the soft voice.

"You here already, Strachan?" he said unnecessarily. He could see the man was here.

"Just one or two things to clear up. Finish the old year before we start the new one, Sir Logan."

Sir Logan nodded with what he hoped was a reasonable degree of affability and went on up the stairs. Damn the man. Why did he make him feel so uncomfortable? Elizabeth didn't like him, he knew, and that worried him a bit. The man was efficient. Attentive. All the things a factor should be. Well, not all . . .

He thought back to last night, and remembered that Strachan had always been in the hall. Now Mackinlay, when he was here, divided his time equally between the band, the hall, and the servants' hall. He was the ideal link man between the house and the estate, which is what he should have been. So ideal that Sir Logan had never noticed until he was no longer there. Now there was someone else with whom to form comparisons, and the comparisons weren't in Strachan's favour.

He heard the green baize door close softly again, and he and Fiona went up to the landing to search for Elizabeth. Dammit, why did he have this uncomfortable feeling that Strachan was biding his time?

10

There had been an Auchtarne High School reunion the previous evening and he'd spent the night with old school friends. It had been pleasant and relaxing, except when they kept asking about Isabel who should have been there as well but wasn't.

The reunion had been fun. He'd drunk more than he should have done, and he'd been louder and more boisterous than he normally was, using the occasion as a kind of safety valve for his frustration.

And now it was the following evening and he'd been deliberately putting off going home until the last possible moment, catching the last bus at the station yard, not wanting to face the silence and the lack of communication in the house. It might take weeks, Wallace had said. It had taken more than that. It was now over six months and there was still no sign of a change in her attitude.

He felt his footsteps getting slower as he approached the house. If anything, it had got worse, because he had become gradually aware that she was wooing Jimmy away from him, spoiling him, offering him bribes to spend more of his time with her, and he knew that if she succeeded in driving this further wedge into their relationship, and if he lost Jimmy's love and companionship, there really would be nothing left to live for.

He looked up at the single light glowing in the bedroom window and sighed before he let himself into the house. There were no lights left on downstairs to welcome him, not even a call from upstairs to ask if he wanted a cup of tea or anything. He went into the living-room and poured himself a very stiff whisky from the bottle in the sideboard and downed it in two gulps. It at least was friendly, sending warmth coursing through his veins, giving him, he thought, strength for what he was about to face.

Reluctantly he climbed the stairs and pushed open the bedroom door. Isabel was lying in bed, a book in front of her. She glanced up at him.

"You've been drinking," she said.

He felt like asking why he shouldn't have been drinking. There wasn't anything else to do.

"Yes —" he began, and then stopped, staring.

Jimmy's cot lay at the bottom of the bed and Jimmy was asleep in it.

"What's this?" he asked.

She turned a page casually.

"Company," she said.

"You know we agreed he should be in his own room."

"Yes."

He felt anger surge in him.

"Then that's where he's going," he said, and he seized the cot and began to wheel it towards the door.

"Leave him alone! Don't you touch him!" she said and he felt pleasure that at last she was showing some kind of emotion.

He paid no attention, simply wheeled the cot across the landing to Jimmy's own room. Jimmy stirred and one small fist went towards his mouth, but he didn't wake up. Brian put the cot back in its rightful place behind the door and left it there, pulling the door to behind him as he came out.

She was standing in the doorway outside their room, her face suffused with anger, her feet bare, her hair in curlers.

"How dare you!" she said

"That's his room. This is ours."

"Well, it won't be for much longer —"

She came for him, her hands bent into claws and he had to seize them to keep them away from his face.

"Stop that!" he said. "For God's sake, Isabel, stop it, stop it, *stop it*!"

She struggled like an animal in a trap and he felt the rage building in him. And also the power. She wasn't as strong as he was. He could do what he liked with her. Make her come to her senses. Force her to return to normality.

She fought in silence, only the shortness of her breath breaking the stillness of the house.

He felt primeval longings in him, the longings of the caveman fighting for his woman, the dominance of the male over the female, and he also felt the white-hot anger burning in him. God in heaven, it was nearly a year since they had made love. How was a man supposed to last that long . . .?

He swung her into his arms and carried her struggling back to the bedroom and threw her on to the bed. She tried to get off, and now she was whimpering softly between heavy breaths, whimpering with fear and he exulted in the thought. He forced her down on to the blankets. Her nightdress had slipped off one shoulder and she tried to pull it back up again, but he knocked her hand away and tore the nightdress off.

He pushed her heavily down on to the bed and began to struggle out of his jacket. While he was fumbling with the buttons of his shirt she managed to slip from under his grasp and got out of the room. He followed her, but stumbled over her slippers, half-hidden under the bed and by the time he had recovered she had reached Jimmy's room and slammed the door and he heard the key turn in the lock.

"Isabel," he whispered. It was strange that even in these circumstances he was unwilling to wake Jimmy. Or maybe it was *because* of these circumstances.

There was no reply but he could hear her distressed whimpering from the other side of the door. There was a startled cry from Jimmy, and he knew she had picked him up and was holding him to her as though for protection.

He slumped against the doorpost, all anger and all lust driven from him now. What a fool. What a fool, to have thought even for a moment that he could force her into submission, bludgeon her back to normality.

The clock in the hall ticked on as though nothing had happened. A little later it struck the half-hour. Half-past twelve.

"Isabel, I'm sorry," he said. "I'm sorry. I shouldn't have —"

"Go away!" the voice hissed from the other side of the door, and at the same time Jimmy began to cry in earnest, a frightened cry, and he heard her crooning to him, comforting him, and a little later the crying stopped and there was silence throughout the house.

He said nothing more, simply stood there for what seemed like an age, and then he went back to the bedroom and threw himself on to the tumbled sheets and blankets, staring unseeingly at the ceiling and wondering what on earth he had done.

11

Donald came down from the hill just as the gloaming was setting in. It had been a wild day with a strong March wind and scuds of rain and it had not been comfortable up on the tops. He was looking forward to getting back to the croft house and the tea which Grace would have prepared for him, and a quiet evening beside the fire. It was pleasant then to listen to the wind moaning round the chimney and know that he hadn't to be out in it again, at least not until the skreigh of day.

It was because he was approaching the croft from an unusual angle that he spotted the intruders before they spotted him. He stopped on the slope and gave a soft whistle to Bess to lie down beside him as he examined the two men who stood beside one of the estate Land Rovers on the track leading to the croft.

Strachan and another man.

Donald frowned. The man with Strachan was about twice Strachan's height and half his weight, a long drink of cold water with wispy hair blowing out from under the brand new deerstalker he wore.

They seemed to be looking towards the croft and he frowned as he whistled to Bess and began to walk down the hill, covering the ground with the long, loping strides which ate up the miles at a most deceptive speed.

He was within fifty yards of them before they became aware of his approach. He saw Strachan catch sight of him and he could almost feel the start he gave. Strachan said something to the man beside him, and then they turned, waiting for him, and Strachan's face broke into a smooth, oily smile.

"Lachlan, how nice to see you," said Strachan.

"Mr Strachan," said Donald non-committally.

"Oh. This is Mr Smith," said Strachan, and Donald noticed the surprised look on the thin, insipid face of the other.

"How do you do, Mr Smith," he said.

"Mr Smith is a friend who has come on a visit," said Strachan, and Donald nodded, wondering why the factor was feeling it necessary to explain Smith's presence.

When Mr Smith spoke his voice was reedy like his appearance and high-pitched and sounded as if he came from Edinburgh.

"What a delightful spot you have for your home, Mr Lachlan," he said. "You must feel very privileged to have such an Arcadian place to live in."

Donald blinked. He hadn't thought of Ardvain in those terms before, and he wasn't sure what Arcadian meant. The place had always been there in his experience, as it had been for his father and his father before him.

"Aye, it's all right," he said.

"I am just taking the opportunity of showing Mr Smith something of Glendarroch," said Strachan.

There he went, explaining things again, and it was funny. The more he explained the less you believed him.

"What a beautiful dog," said Mr Smith, looking at the wet and bedraggled Bess who looked anything but beautiful at the moment. He bent his long length to fondle her, but Bess backed away with a low growl. Donald had always known Bess had good taste.

"Heel, lass," he said quietly, and Bess came and lay down at his feet, watching the two men with wary eyes.

"Well," said Strachan. "We must get on. It'll be dark soon."

They turned back to the Land Rover and Donald watched them.

"Good day to you, Lachlan," said Strachan.

"Good day," said Donald.

"A pleasure to have met you, Mr Lachlan," said the man Strachan had called Smith and he bent himself to get into the Land Rover and Donald stood watching as it drove off down the track towards Glendarroch.

Then he whistled to Bess and strode the last quarter of a mile home, wondering what Strachan had been doing up there with a long drink of water like the man he had called Smith. Whatever it was, he was sure it wouldn't have been for his good.

12

He had never walked into a bar with the fixed intention of getting drunk before, but this time his mind was firmly made up. It had been from the time he stepped on to the bus in Glendarroch until he got off at the Auchtarne Arms and made deliberately for the cocktail bar, not the public, because there was always the chance that there might be someone in there who knew him. Not that he really cared whether anyone saw him or not. In the present state of affairs, such an event was of minor importance.

The cocktail bar of the Auchtarne Arms became busy in the summer months when the tourists used it, but in April it was very quiet and he went and sat in an easy chair in an inconspicuous corner.

A waitress came and he ordered a large whisky and she brought it on a tray with a jug of water. He drank it quickly and ordered another one, waiting for the familiar easing effect to creep over him.

There was no one else in the cocktail bar. Just the barman in a white jacket behind the bar and the waitress who spent most of her time leaning on the bar talking to him in low tones, occasionally laughing at something the man said.

The soothing effect of the whisky seemed a long time coming this evening. The same familiar thoughts kept tramping around in his head without fading as they usually did after a drink.

Isabel and Jimmy in *their* bedroom. The bedroom *he* had the right to occupy with *her*. And in those circumstances Jimmy was naturally becoming a mummy's boy, to the exclusion of himself. That was what hurt. Isabel seemed reluctant to allow Jimmy to have anything to do with him now. He was an outcast in his own home. No wife. No son . . .

Well, to hell with them both.

He held up his hand and the waitress spotted it and came towards him.

"Another one," he said.

She smiled at him, a warm, understanding smile, and turned back to the bar. He watched her hips sway as she went. She was young and fresh-looking, quite pretty, with a good figure. Too much make-up and the hair not very well groomed, but pleasant looking . . .

She brought the drink back to him and bent over to put it down. Her black dress was very low cut.

"Have one yourself?" he said suddenly on the spur of the moment.

"Thanks," she said. "I'll save it for afters. When I'm off duty."

He handed her another ten shilling note and she returned to the bar.

He lost count of how much he drank, though it seemed to have no effect on him, and it was a surprise when the barman suddenly called last orders. He looked at the clock and realised that the last bus to Glendarroch had gone ten minutes ago.

Well, what do we do now? he asked himself as he got to his feet and felt the cocktail bar spin slightly as he did so. The floor seemed to billow like the waves on the shore of the loch after a storm, and he put out a hand and grasped a chair-back to steady himself.

"All right, pet?" a soft voice said in his ear and he felt his arm gripped and the touch sent a tingle of pleasure rippling through him.

"Yes. Fine. Perffily all right," he said, finding it curiously difficult to form words.

But he was very conscious of the arm on his, and with an effort he put one of his arms round her waist, purely for additional support. It was narrow and firm and he felt a stir of longing in him.

"Better get away home to your bed, pet," she said as she opened the door of the cocktail bar and propelled him gently on to the pavement.

"Haven gorra bed," he mumbled, but the door closed behind him and he was alone on the dark pavement, alone in Auchtarne. Alone in the world with nowhere to go.

13

They sat in the Land Rover and watched the smoke rise from the chimney in a straight line into the still, bright air. It wouldn't be long now before the leaves on the tree in the yard down there began to bloom, covering the branches in a brilliant green blanket.

Strachan finished polishing his glasses, put them on again and turned to Mr Smith.

"You're sure this is the one?" he asked.

Mr Smith nodded.

"Oh, yes," he said. "This is by far the best. It would be ideal. The peace. The beauty."

"Aye," said Strachan. "The lone shieling and the misty island. I know. Have you thought about the winters?"

"Frequently," said Mr Smith. "Snug inside with a log fire going, and a fresh notebook and a pen. Ah, I could pass my days here very easily, Mr Strachan."

"Well, it's certainly the best situated and the best maintained. All right. If you're sure."

"You mean if *you're* sure. I understand that crofters have security of tenure. They can't be forced out."

"That's perfectly true. They can't. But there's nothing to stop them from giving up their crofts. They frequently do. Go to some more profitable occupation in the town. Or a lot of them go to sea, you know."

"And you feel that is what will happen here?"

Strachan smiled.

"Oh, yes. But it may take time."

"How long?"

"Difficult to say. A year. Maybe two."

"That would be entirely suitable. As you know, I don't retire from St Andrew's House until the end of next year. I should not want anything till then. But after that . . . Ah, after that, Mr Strachan! Dear me, it won't be the occasional poem after *that*. Oh, no. There is so much in my head just waiting to come out, and it's in a place like this it will have the best chance to develop."

Strachan grunted. He knew nothing about his companion's literary aspirations beyond the fact that he had shown him what he called some verses published in *The Scotsman*. They didn't mean much to Strachan. He couldn't understand what the words meant and he didn't see any reason for breaking what he'd written into short and long lines, but he supposed Smith knew what he was doing.

"Right. Leave it to me," he said. "We'll keep in touch."

He started the engine, reversed the Land Rover into an entry to a field and turned down the track back to Glendarroch.

14

"You look an absolute mess," said Maggie as Brian passed her on the way off the bus.

He stopped and turned to her. He was unshaven, his hair hadn't been combed and his eyes were bloodshot. He wasn't in the best of tempers either.

"Have you looked at yourself recently?" he asked.

"Don't you dare —" she began

"Shut your big, gossiping mouth, you lousy old bag," he said.

"How dare you speak to me like that?"

"Who started this conversation, anyway?"

She gaped at him, unable to believe her ears and she missed the chance of retaliation, because by the time she'd recovered her senses he'd gone, heading for the house behind the store.

Quivering with indignation, Maggie switched off the engine and prepared to follow him, at least as far as the shop, where she knew Isabel would be waiting with the usual cup of tea, and she could tell her exactly what her husband had said to her.

She'd noticed over the last few weeks that when she said something critical about Brian Isabel didn't object. Gradually her criticisms had become more pointed and obvious and still there was no protest. Maggie would have liked to ask if things were going wrong between them, but she didn't want to do that. For one thing, actually knowing would take away a lot of the pleasure of finding more critical things to say about him.

But now she had a real reason for indignation.

She had given him a lift into Auchtarne yesterday afternoon but he hadn't been on the bus back. Last night the last train had been on time and so she'd been able to leave the station square at a reasonable hour and he'd evidently missed her. That was why he was on the first run back to Glendarroch this morning. By the look of him he'd slept rough, probably in the Memorial Park.

But why, that was what Maggie wanted to know, still seething with indignation at the way he had spoken to her, and she wondered if she could pump any information out of Isabel.

15

"But it's less than a year since the last rise!" said Donald, aghast at what Strachan had just told him.

Strachan nodded sympathetically, leaning out of the window of the Land Rover.

"I know exactly how you feel, Lachlan. But you must realise how inflation is hitting the estate these days. You wouldn't believe the way costs are rising."

"You don't need to tell me," said Donald with feeling.

"Well, there you are, then," said Strachan as though that settled everything. "It's at times like these that we all have to draw in our belts, isn't it?"

Donald grunted and looked out across the hills which had been his home, wondering how much longer they would continue to be so. The hours were long, the work was hard, the return pitiful, yet it was the only life he had ever known, the only life he cared to think about. If it wasn't for this — the sheep on the hills and the crops in the fields, birth and growth and the changing of seasons — what else would there be?

"I'll need to see Sir Logan," he muttered.

Strachan smiled again. The sunlight glinted on his glasses, so Donald couldn't see how far the smile reached. Not very far, he thought.

"Oh, I don't think I'd bother Sir Logan if I were you," he said. "Sir Logan has troubles enough of his own. I won't go into details, but you understand, I'm sure, Lachlan, that running the estate these days is a ticklish business."

"He'd understand my position," said Donald, thinking of how the rents had risen over the last few years while the income had stayed virtually the same. He was no mathematician, no accountant, he didn't really understand figures, but he knew enough to understand when the outgoings exceeded the incomings and were going to get higher.

"You think I don't know?" said Strachan. "Believe me, Lachlan, I do. And I've been wondering whether there isn't anything I can do to help you."

"You could help me by keeping the rent down," said Donald.

"Unfortunately that's outside my sphere of influence, you understand."

"You're the factor. It's your job."

"I know, I know, but I'm also at the beck and call of others. Accountants, tax inspectors, all the rest of them. Now, I wouldn't mention this to everyone around here, but I know you, Lachlan, and I know the sort of chap you are. I have several influential friends in Glasgow. And I know they're always on the lookout for reliable, hard-working fellows like yourself —"

Donald shook his head and took a breath to speak, but Strachan held up a hand.

"No. Hear me out," he said. "Wouldn't that be better all round? A good steady job with a good steady wage, some future for your son and a comfortable life for your wife? Isn't that worth thinking about?"

"No," said Donald with a great deal more heat than he had meant, but the picture Strachan was raising in his mind, of a city street, a factory floor, of enclosure and no fresh air, no hills to walk over, no wide open vistas to rest your eyes on, filled him with a nameless foreboding. Anything would be better than that.

"No," he said again. "I'd never agree to that."

Strachan's smile became slightly fixed.

"I think you should," he said. "Don't decide anything on the spur of the moment. Talk it over with your family. Then come and see me, I can promise you I'll do everything in my power to help you."

He nodded encouragingly, slipped the Land Rover into gear and moved off down the road, leaving Donald looking after him with a black cloud of depression in his mind and a pain at his heart.

16

Isabel hadn't let Jimmy attend the funeral. Logically Brian knew this to be right. The side of a grave was no place for a four-year-old boy, and he wouldn't have wanted him to be there himself.

But it would have been nice to be consulted. After all, it was his mother's funeral and Jimmy was his son, too.

And after the service, after he and David had thrown the little clods of dry earth on to the polished top of the coffin and turned away, she had hurried off to Mrs Woods's cottage, where she had left Jimmy, without a word.

Brian stared out of the window of the bus as Graham Ferguson drove it towards Auchtarne. In the seat in front of him sat David and Helen, talking in low voices, an intimate conversation such as he never had now.

And his mother had gone to join his father. She wasn't old, he thought. Just worn out. She'd had enough after sixty-four years and didn't see the point in going on any longer.

He found himself sympathising with her.

Graham turned the bus into the station square at Auchtarne and they got off. David and Helen gathered their luggage from the compartment at the back and they went on to the platform and crossed the bridge over the rails to the other side.

There were a few holidaymakers waiting for the train back to Glasgow. The sun shone brilliantly from a clear August sky, and they stood, saying nothing, wishing the train would hurry up so that this final embarrassing parting would be over.

It came at last, only ten minutes late, and David and Helen got aboard. He stood on the platform as David lowered the carriage window and leant out.

"Keep in touch," he said, and Brian nodded.

The guard's whistle blew and the engine belched steam and the train began to move. Helen waved from inside the carriage and David stayed leaning out until a bend in the line hid him from view and there was nothing of them left except the two silver threads curving away into the distance.

Brian stood for a while until the last rumble of the train faded. That was that, he thought, and resolutely pushed regret and nostalgia away from him. He crossed the bridge again and walked through the little booking hall out into the yard.

The bus back to Glendarroch stood there glistening in the sunshine, but there was no sign of Graham. He was glad it had been Graham driving. There had been no questions and there would be no interest shown in what he was doing or why he wasn't on the homeward journey as there would have been with Maggie.

Because he wasn't going to go back. Not yet, anyway.

He turned out of the yard, his feet taking him without

thought towards the Auchtarne Arms. He walked slowly, deliberately, his mind full of depressing thoughts.

She hadn't said anything to him during the service or during the actual burial. She hadn't touched him to comfort him in his bereavement. Simply stood beside him because it was her duty to do so. And she wouldn't ask him why he was late home. She simply didn't care.

He turned into the cocktail bar of the Auchtarne Arms just as the town clock struck five.

"Hello, Brian," she said. "Here, I was awful sorry to hear about your Mum."

"Thanks, Avril," he said.

Here at least there was sympathy. She brought him a large whisky without his even having to ask for it and she sat down in the seat opposite him in her low-cut dress, cupped her chin in her hands and looked at him out of over-made-up eyes which in his present state of numbness and loneliness seemed to be soft and gentle and full of care.

"An old lady, was she?" she asked.

He suddenly found himself pouring out stories of his mother and himself, things he hadn't really thought about for years, but which came back to him now with sudden clarity. He wasn't really aware of her, except that she was a soft voice and a sympathetic ear. He had met her several times since that first time when she'd helped him out of the Auchtarne Arms at closing time and he'd missed the bus and spent a cold and uncomfortable night in the bandstand at the Memorial Park. Her name was Avril Hendry and she came from Dundee. This was only a holiday job but she was good at it and attracted the customers and the manager had asked her to take a permanent job here but she hadn't made up her mind about that yet. He'd found himself hoping that she would stay on. He'd come to look forward to his visits to the cocktail bar, and she seemed to look forward to him being there.

That was all she was, he told himself. A voice and an ear. At the end of each evening he had said a polite and careful goodnight to her before making sure that he caught the last bus home. But on the day his mother was buried he had had this visit planned in the back of his mind from the very beginning, plotting the times of getting David and Helen to the station, then slipping down to the Auchtarne Arms instead of going home because he knew that there he could get a little comfort, not only from the whisky bottle but from Avril as well.

17

It was getting late. Dougal had retired to bed half an hour ago, since he would be out on the hill at daybreak tomorrow.

Donald pushed the books and papers away from him with a sigh of distaste. From her seat by the fire Grace looked up from her knitting.

Their eyes met. He could see the worry in hers and he felt comforted by that. These last few weeks he had felt as though care and worry were building leaden weights into his boots. He had never before found walking over the hills to be an effort. Now it was beginning to be so and he resented it, especially as he was pretty sure he knew the reason why it was happening.

"We can't go on like this," he said.

"Is it that bad?" asked Grace.

"We're eating into our savings and God kens there's not much of them," said Donald.

"You'll need to see Sir Logan," said Grace.

"Aye, I ken. But it's not so easy. Sir Logan never comes up to these parts now. He's getting on a bit. And if I go down to the Big House there's aye the man Strachan hanging about, keeping me away from him."

He stared gloomily into the fire for a few minutes. Beyond the window the October night was dark and still, waiting for the onset of winter, and after that happened they would be virtually cut off up here until the spring. . . . It was the time for laying in stores to withstand what might be a long siege, but that meant money to pay for them. Without it starvation could very well be just round the corner.

They could do it. Just. But it would leave nothing over for

emergencies. Emergencies like yet another rent rise in the spring.

"You've got to get past Strachan somehow," said Grace.

"Aye, but how? If I write Sir Logan a letter Strachan gets it first. And I'm no hand at the writing, as you know. And I can't go down to the road end and use the telephone box for the calls go straight through to Strachan too. And it's him that's turning the screws, I ken that."

Grace took up her knitting again and for a moment there was silence except for the click-clicking of the pins.

"It'll be as bad for the other crofters," she said at last. "At least you're not on your lea-lane."

"Aye," said Donald with a note of doubt in his voice which she picked up.

"You think that's not so?" she asked.

"Oh, they've had their rents put up too," he said. "There's no doubt of that. But from what I can gather their rise hasn't been as bad as ours."

"Are you sure?"

"No, I'm not. You know what the folk around here are like when it comes to talking about money. They shut up like clams. No one'll give you a straight answer. But from one or two things I've picked up I don't think they're suffering the way we're suffering."

He picked up the account book from the table and looked helplessly from it to the figures he had been scrawling laboriously on a sheet of paper all evening.

"And I wonder why he's doing it," he said.

18

Strachan took off his glasses, put the ledger away in the bottom drawer of his desk, locked the drawer, put the key in his pocket and sat back, tapping his teeth with the forefinger of each hand.

It wasn't as good as he would have liked.

He stared out of the window without seeing anything. When he put his glasses back on again he saw that the short winter day had already drawn to a close so there was nothing to see there anyway.

Money. Money. Money . . .

It should be all right, he thought. By careful planning he was able to keep ahead, but for how long? And there was a limit to the number of times he could put the rents up. There had been a lot of squalling about that already.

So long as he could get the Lachlan croft vacated by the end of this year. That gave him ten and a half months. Well, the pressure should have worked by then.

After that, "Smith" would take the place over, and the rent from that croft would double.

Not as far as the estate books were concerned, of course. But it would make a very handy little bit of extra to put in his pocket and ease this chronic shortage.

Yes. It was all right. At the moment. And Peddie was getting older and less interested in the minutiae of running the estate. And the daughter didn't take much interest either. Who knew what there might not be available at the end of the day?

19

It had been a fine early spring night when he set off from Auchtarne, but halfway back the rain began to fall and he hunched his shoulders over the handlebars as he drove the pedals round.

His mind was confused, battered into numbness.

He hadn't meant to do it. It was all a mistake. He hadn't even asked her to. All they'd done was leave the Auchtarne Arms at closing time and walk the silent streets, saying nothing. She'd put an arm through his and he'd drawn her to him, pressing her against him, feeling warmth and comfort in the contact and she'd seemed to understand his need.

"Come on, pet," she'd said softly at last and she turned his steps back towards the Auchtarne Arms. It must have been late, for the lights were all out. There were few guests so early in the season, but she lived in and had a key to the back door.

She'd led him through the silent kitchen to the front hall and up the dark stairs. She'd opened one of the vacant bedroom doors and pulled him in, locking the door behind her.

And it was only at that point that he really admitted to himself that he needed her. Admitted it before she pulled back the bedcover and started undressing in front of him.

He could have said no. Thank you very much but not tonight, I've got other things to do. I've got a wife and child at home. It's very kind of you, but no thanks.

But he hadn't said any of those things.

The bicycle met an upward gradient and he changed gear and set his legs pumping harder to maintain his momentum up the slope. The rain fell, not heavily, but with a gentle persistence.

Afterwards he'd lain on his back while she smoked a cigarette beside him and he wondered exactly what he had done and what effect it would have on his life. Would things ever be the same at home again? Could he look Jimmy in the face? It was different with Isabel, because she never looked him in the face now anyway, but until now *he'd* always been able to look at *her*. Avril had slipped out of the bed and dressed again and then left the room. She returned in a couple of minutes with clean sheets and pillowcases, and he wondered briefly how she could be so practised, know precisely what to do.

It had all been a ghastly mistake. It should never have happened . . .

The bicycle reached the top of the hill and he began to freewheel down the slope which led to Glendarroch, the dynamo whining on the back wheel behind him and the headlight cutting a little shaft of light ahead, enough to see the edge of the road.

Stop kidding yourself, he thought disgustedly. Be honest. You knew it was going to happen. You've been wanting it to happen for weeks. You just didn't have the guts to initiate it yourself. You had to wait for her to do it all. Why else did you buy this second-hand bike? You've never been a cyclist. It was simply to get in and out of Auchtarne at night without Maggie seeing you on the bus and spreading the news all over the village.

And in spite of his misgivings and his pangs of conscience, he knew that as Avril lay in his arms he had experienced an enormous sense of relief.

He dismounted at the back of the deserted garage where old Richards used to do a desultory trade in repairs and forced the rickety door open as quietly as he could, wheeled the bike in and chained it to the leg of the rough bench inside. Then he left the garage, pulled the door closed behind him and stood in the gentle smirr of rain without being aware of it. Relief, yes, he thought. But not emotional comfort.

There was no comfort. There was no comfort anywhere.

20

The Big House pew had seemed strangely empty today.

Sir Logan tried to remember when the last time was that he had been to church without Dorothy and he found it hard to think. It had been a long time ago, anyway, and he'd felt conspicuous sitting in that pew all on his own. No Dorothy. No Elizabeth. Dammit, things were falling apart round his ears....

He shook hands with MacPherson at the door as he led the way out.

"I hope Lady Peddie improves, Sir Logan," said Mac-Pherson.

"Thanks, Padre, I hope so too. Good sermon, that. Well done," said Sir Logan and he headed down the path to the gate beyond which stood the Armstrong-Siddeley.

"Sir Logan, could I have a word with you, please?"

It was Lachlan. Donald Lachlan. One of the crofters up at Ardvain. Good chap, Lachlan, but he wished he'd found a better time to speak.

"Yes, all right, Lachlan, but don't take too long will you?" he said a little testily, looking round for Syme who had not yet emerged from the church. Others were pouring out into the spring sunshine.

Wallace doesn't seem happy about Dorothy, he thought. Wants her to go into hospital for some sort of tests. Dammit, that just means the quack doesn't know what the matter is and wants someone else to find out. I wonder if I should ask for a second opinion myself? Get a man up from Edinburgh to have a look at the old girl, tell me what's really the matter? Save poor old Dorothy going into hospital. She'd hate that. Specially now, with the flowers at their best. Lost so much weight, poor old thing. Not much stamina left in her, either. . . .

Lachlan was burbling away about being put out of his croft but he wasn't really listening.

"That's rubbish, Lachlan," he said a little shortly. "No one can put you out of your croft. You know that as well as I do, man."

"I know that, Sir Logan. That's what I'm saying. But I may be forced to leave, that's the trouble."

"Now look here, Lachlan, you're a good man. One of the best I've got up there. And I'm not going to let you go, you understand?"

"You mean it, Sir Logan?"

"Of course I mean it. Dammit, it's people like you who are the backbone of the estate."

Here was Syme now, hurrying down the path. He unlocked the door and Sir Logan climbed in, feeling it strange to have the back seat to himself. Funny how he missed Dorothy. Always taken her for granted, he supposed. Only when she wasn't there that you noticed she was missing. He wound down the window.

"Cheer up, Lachlan," he said as Syme climbed into the driving seat and started the engine. "You're safe as houses up there."

The car moved off and left Lachlan standing there not looking terribly convinced, and Sir Logan sank back into the seat. What had the man said? Muttered something about Strachan, didn't he? That man again . . .

He hoped Mrs Syme had prepared something good and tasty for lunch, something Dorothy would appreciate and maybe eat for a change.

Dammit, the old girl would have to get better soon. The summer was here and the roses were needing her attention in the garden.

21

It was the first time Wallace had seen Brian Blair in his surgery. That in itself warned him that the Blairs' problem was entering a new phase, a suspicion confirmed by what Brian was saying and from the desperation behind it. It wasn't simply a problem with Isabel now. It was a problem which concerned Brian personally as well, though Brian was saying nothing about himself.

"It sounds to me as though she should see a psychiatrist," he said when Brian eventually fell silent. "Do you think that would help her?"

"I'm sure it would," said Brian. "But I don't know how we could get her to do it."

"She wouldn't go if you asked her to? Explained why she ought to?"

"Doctor, if I asked her to go to see a psychiatrist I think she would blow her top completely. I'm the last person to get her to do anything at the moment."

Wallace nodded. From the personal problems the Blairs were having and as Brian had explained them to him, he could understand that. He sighed to himself. He had found there were many unpleasant sides to the practice of medicine since joining his father here in Auchtarne.

"Would you like me to sound her out?"

The reply was inevitable.

"Would you, Doctor?"

"Certainly. But I'm not going to rush it. It would be better if we waited for a chance for me to call, maybe when I'm in the village, just for a chat in passing, wouldn't you think?"

Brian nodded eagerly.

"That would do it," he said. "I'd be very grateful. It's gone on too long. I — it can't go on much longer. It really can't."

After Brian had left, Wallace tapped thoughtfully at the notes which started in his father's untidy, spidery hand and continued in his own which wasn't any better.

He understood the need to get Isabel to a psychiatrist. That had been growing more and more necessary as the months passed. What worried him at the moment was the underlying impression of guilt which he had got from Brian himself and he hoped the obvious cause wasn't the correct one. . . .

22

"There you are, Hector, you sign the paper. Just there, Mr Strachan?"

"That is correct, Mrs Mack. Just there."

"Just there, Hector."

"Yes, dear," he said as he took the pen from her and signed his name. He handed the pen back to the smiling man and wondered whether he had done the right thing.

They now had the lease of one of the cottages in the village as from the end of the year. In six months he would retire from the ticket office at St Enoch Station and they would move to Glendarroch.

He didn't look forward to either event with much pleasure.

His work had been his life. He had enjoyed it and he had been good at it. Perhaps he hadn't progressed so far in the railway service as he might have expected when he first started as a lad all those years ago, especially when, with his feet, he had been rejected for service during the war. That was the time when he ought, perhaps, to have gained promotion, but he had been tied to Auchtarne for longer than was normal while his mother was alive. He wasn't sure that he looked forward to being in this cottage after he retired. It was very small. There really would be very little chance of escape.

That was the wrong way to think about it. But he didn't really want to come to Glendarroch. After selling the bungalow in Pollokshaws it would have been easy to buy a small place in Auchtarne and have a bit left over, and if they had settled there he could have strolled down to the station every now and again. Perhaps they'd let him sit in the ticket office in front of the stove in the winter months to watch the trains come and go and remember the old days. . . . He understood there were diesel locomotives starting on the line soon. . . .

And quite apart from his own feelings in the matter he wasn't sure whether this cottage was a good idea. He knew why Mary wanted it. She wanted to keep an eye on her sister because, she was always telling him, Lizzie wasn't quite right in the head.

But Lizzie always seemed perfectly all right in the head to him, right from that night he had first met her in the station yard and offered her a lift to Glendarroch on his scooter. The scooter had gone long ago, because Mary said they were noisy and dangerous and no doubt she was right. But Lizzie hadn't had a tizzie that night and he noticed that Lizzie's tizzies only happened when Mary was there and it seemed to him that the two sisters rubbed each other up the wrong way. Hector wondered how Lizzie would fare if her sister was within such easy and permanent reach.

Oh, well, it was done now. He'd signed the lease and the cottage would be theirs from 1st January 1966.

Mr Strachan accompanied them to the back door of Glendarroch House and ushered them out, shaking hands with each of them as they went.

"What a charming man," said Mary as they walked down the drive towards the village. "So polite and helpful, wasn't he, Hector?"

"Yes, dear."

"I think I'm going to enjoy living here," said Mary, surveying the village as they walked up the main street with the neat cottages on either side. "There is going to be so much for me to do."

Hector sighed, but quietly.

"Yes, dear," he said.

"Come along, then, Hector. There will just be time for us to have a cup of tea at the manse with Lizzie before we have to catch the bus back to Auchtarne. I just hope it won't be that dreadful vulgar woman driving it again. She is quite likely to land us in the ditch and then we might miss the train home."

"Yes, dear," said Hector.

23

"How is he, Doctor?" asked Brian as Wallace came through to the shop.

"It's measles," said Wallace. "A lot of it about at the moment. He's got a slight temperature but it's a mild attack and there's nothing to worry about."

Brian raised his eyebrows in a question, and Wallace casually pushed the door into the house closed behind him.

"Isabel's tucking him up again," he said, then lowered his voice. "No good, I'm afraid. You were right. She won't think of it. Tensed up as soon as I mentioned the subject."

"I told you," said Brian.

"We'll have to think of something else," said Wallace. "You're quite right. She needs help. And badly."

He crossed to the shop door and opened it.

"I'll drop in again tomorrow," he said. "Maybe we can talk again then after I've had a chance to think about it. Must rush. I'm due at the Big House in ten minutes."

"Lady Peddie?" asked Brian.

"Yes. Poor soul," said Wallace. "Sir Logan's sent for another man from Edinburgh. He wants a second opinion. It's not a second opinion, though. It's a fourth. And the opinion will be the same as the other three, I'm afraid." And he was gone, closing the door behind him.

"Did you set him up?"

He whirled round. Isabel stood in the doorway behind the post office counter.

"What do you mean?"

"All that talk about me seeing a doctor. I know what kind of doctor he was talking about. Not an ordinary doctor, was it? A mental doctor, that's what he was on about."

She spoke quietly but with a wealth of venom in her voice.

"Listen, we just thought you needed help, that's all."

"So you start plotting behind my back, is that it? I don't need help. And don't you start trying to do things when I'm not looking, do you hear me?"

"Isabel, for God's sake, can't you see —"

"All I can see is what you've done to me. And you've done enough. And I'm not having any more, do you hear me?"

"I hear you all right, but I don't know what you're on about. I wish I did. Look, could we not just have a quiet, reasonable talk about it? Like we used to . . ."

She laughed without an atom of humour.

"Oh, the old days, is it? When we were young and innocent and life was all wonderful?"

"Well, it was . . ."

"It never was. It was always disgusting and horrible and — and — oh, go away!"

She whirled round and disappeared and he leant on the counter with his head in his hands wondering where on earth they were going to go from here.

24

"But this is the third dinner party this month!" said Elizabeth.

"Second," said Peter.

"Well, all right. The Frasers and the Masons were at the end of May. It's still three dinner parties in four weeks."

"Elizabeth, it's very important, you know. If I'm to get a partnership in Wishart and Law I do need to entertain the bosses. Introduce you to them. Let them see how we live and who and what we are."

"Oh, I can tell you what I am all right," said Elizabeth angrily. "I'm a skivvy. That's what I am. Spending my days looking after Fiona, trying to cook meals, trying to serve them, washing the dishes, ironing your shirts. It's non-stop and I'm sick and fed up with it."

"Please keep your voice down. They'll hear you next door."

He indicated the open window through which she could see the children playing in the park. They might have been the same children she had seen that day, that happy day, more than four years ago when she had come back after learning that she was pregnant. But no, they couldn't be. Those ones would have grown by now. This would be another lot.

"Oh, they'll hear us next door. They'll hear us downstairs. They'll hear us on the roof. They're on top of you everywhere. I'm fed up with it!"

She was being unreasonable, she knew, but she felt this tantrum was doing her good, getting rid of some of the pent-up frustration she had been feeling recently. And it was true. More and more she was finding Edinburgh claustrophobic, the crowds, the nearness of the houses, the numbers of people, most of whom seemed to have to be entertained to dinner. . . .

"Elizabeth, be reasonable. Honestly, this is the last time for as far as I can foresee. You do realise that if I get this partnership it'll make a big difference to us financially? We could move to a bigger house. More isolated. More what you're used to."

She sighed and sat down on the sofa.

"There's not much point in that," she said. "It would just be that much easier to burgle. I'm sorry, Peter. I really am. I just feel — I don't know —"

But she did know, only she couldn't say it to him. This wasn't the place for her. She wasn't bred to the city. It was strange to her. Oh, it was all right for a visit, but hell to live in. And the proof of that was in these arguments they had. They were becoming more and more frequent and what was worse, they were becoming more and more bitter . . .

"It's all right, Elizabeth. Tell you what. We could take them out to the Café Royal or something."

"Six people? That's too expensive. And it doesn't show you off in your own home, which is what you want, isn't it?" she said.

She noticed the whiteness round his nostrils, which was a sure sign of anger.

"You want servants again, is that it?" he said. "Just like you've been used to all your life."

"How dare you!"

The telephone rang in the hall and after a moment he went to answer it.

She sat back and closed her eyes, wondering what on earth she was going to do.

After a while she realised that Peter wasn't speaking, and she turned to look at him. He was listening and his face had turned very serious. He saw her looking at him and he turned away as though he didn't want her to hear what was being said. After a moment he murmured something into the receiver which sounded like "I'll tell her" and put it down. He stood quite still for a moment then she saw him square his shoulders and he turned and came back into the sitting-room.

"Peter — what is it?" she asked, suddenly frightened by the look on his face.

"I'm sorry, Elizabeth," he said. "That was Dr Wallace . . ."

She felt her heart turn cold.

"Mother —?" she asked.

He nodded.

"She died an hour ago," he said.

25

They kept telling her that Granny had gone away so Fiona couldn't quite understand why they were going to Glendarroch. That was where Granny always was, but if *she'd* gone away why did *they* have to go there? And if she *wasn't* there, where *was* she? Granny was *always* at Glendarroch. She tried to ask when Granny was coming home again, but no one would answer that question. They'd just say again that Granny had gone away which wasn't much help.

When they got out of the car at the Big House which she loved so much, Dandad was waiting on the steps. She ran to him and he picked her up and hugged her to him very hard and kissed her so that his bristly moustache tickled her cheek.

"Thank you for coming, little mouse," he said, and she saw there were tears in his eyes. Or maybe they were just watering in the bright summer sunlight. He held her hand very tightly as they all walked into the house.

Everything seemed unusually quiet. The grown-ups kept

talking in low voices as she played with Mummy's old doll's house on the drawing-room carpet. She couldn't hear what they were saying but she could see that they kept looking at her and she wondered if they were talking about Granny, who certainly wasn't here.

It was lovely being back in her old room over the front door and waking to the sunlight trying to burst its way through the curtains. Later she sat in the church, hardly able to see over the pew, and listened to the minister saying words which she didn't understand. She spent most of the time looking round the church which was full of people in very dark clothes, mostly black, some with funny black hats, and those that didn't wear black clothes had black bands round their sleeves.

There was a big box in the middle of the church too, a long, shiny box with a bright golden label on the top which she couldn't see properly from where she was sitting, and she looked at it with wonder because she'd never seen a box just there in the church before. She sat between Mummy and Daddy and wondered what it was for. Dandad sat just beside Mummy and they were all dressed in black too. There were lots of other people in the pews just behind who had shaken her solemnly by the hand before they left the Big House for the church and had said: "So this is Fiona."

Mummy had called them names like Uncle William and Auntie Barbara but the names didn't mean anything to her and she didn't remember ever having seen them before.

But they were all here, and after they'd all stood up and sung another hymn, four men came and picked up the box and carried it out of the church. Then everyone began to follow the men and the box, but Daddy took her hand and said, "Come on, Fiona, we'll go for a walk, shall we?"

"Isn't Mummy coming too?"

"In a little while."

She went reluctantly, because that box was very important and she wanted to know what was in it and what was going to happen to it now, but she knew that this wasn't the time or the place to make a fuss so she went obediently with Daddy. They went out by a side door and along one of the paths to the gate, and she began to skip, feeling somehow freer than she had felt in the church, which was a funny place to be anyway because it wasn't Sunday.

They walked down to the shore of the loch and she threw stones into the still water, watching the ripples spread out and she felt the summer sun warm on her face. She wondered why Granny would want to go away just now when she could have been here in this lovely place in the warm summer sunshine.

Later, as Daddy drove Mummy and her back towards the Big House, following the black car which Dandad was being driven in, she heard Mummy say something about tomorrow . . .

"Are we going home tomorrow?" she asked.

Mummy turned to her from the front seat where she was sitting beside Daddy.

"No, darling," she said. "Daddy's going back tomorrow because Daddy's got a lot of work to do. But you and I will stay here for a little while."

"Goodie!" she said and she saw Mummy and Daddy glance at each other.

"You'll have to help to keep Dandad cheerful," said Mummy.

"Yes, I will," she said. "We'll go for lots of walks, won't we? And see the horses and the cows and the sheep and have picnics and things. It'll be lovely!"

She wasn't sure, but she thought she heard Daddy sigh as he turned the car through the gates leading to the Big House.

Chapter Three
1966-1969
1

"Brian."

He grunted

"We got to talk."

He turned over and lay looking up at the ceiling. He noticed that the cornice ran round the window and the wall which contained the door, then suddenly stopped at the corner where the room had been partitioned to form two smaller rooms from one very big one. They must have used every room in the hotel by now, he thought, with some disgust.

"You listening, pet?"

He grunted again.

"How long we gonny go on like this?"

He was beginning to ask himself the same question.

"I've been good to you, haven't I not?"

He felt her hand stroking his hair, and he grunted again in acknowledgement. It was strange how difficult it was to talk to her.

"What sort of an answer is that? I've aye given you what you wanted, eh no?"

A grunt wouldn't suffice any longer. He turned and looked at her where she lay propped up on one elbow, her other hand stretched out to ruffle his hair.

"Yes, Avril, you have," he said with some reluctance.

"There. I kent you'd say that. Well, listen, pet, I've been thinkin'. What about you and me gettin' hitched, eh? Makin' a proper go of it. I don't know about you, but I'm gettin' bloody scunnered at all these hotel rooms."

He turned away again, feeling some revulsion. Dawn was breaking and the first faint March light was outlining the window. They never closed the curtains, nor did they ever switch on the light in case the manager happened to see the window from outside and wonder why the room was occupied when there was no one in the register. But the growing daylight had shown her sufficiently clearly to him, her face still covered in last night's heavy make-up, unwashed, sour looking, her dark hair which in the early days had seemed so bewitchingly full and lush, looking greasy and tangled.

Was it fair on her that, having used her all these months to satisfy his basic animal instincts, he now found her to be cheap and tawdry, utterly repugnant — her conversation trite, her attitude of mind sordid, her whole being shallow and uninteresting?

No, it wasn't her fault that she was as she was. It was his that he had been attracted to her in the first place, that he had allowed his own loneliness and frustration to blind him to the obvious facts, had used her in a way which had given her a hold over him so that now she saw her way to a security which she would otherwise never have. He was the owner of Blair's Store at Glendarroch, maybe not a goldmine but at least a hedge against inflation and old age.

God, what had he done?

He gripped the edge of the sheet, crushing it in his fists as he tried to fight his way out of a situation entirely of his own making.

"I mean, pet, she's no good to you, is she? You've said so. Well, get rid of her. That's not difficult, you ken. I mean, we can just go on doin' what we're doin' now, only we register properly and give her the receipt, know what I mean? There's her proof. You don't need to do anythin' different. Divorce is easy now. Then we can get hitched and live happily ever after."

She snuggled up against his back, pressing herself to him, and he caught a whiff of stale, cheap perfume.

"Hey," she said suddenly. "Watch what you're doin'. That's a hotel sheet you're rippin' apart."

2

The old Peddie headstone had been full, so Sir Logan had ordered a new one. It was large and ornate and it had finally been erected yesterday over Lady Peddie's grave. Strachan had thought it a good idea to come down this morning to make sure it was in the right place and that everything was as it should be, because he knew that Sir Logan intended to come and look at it himself after the church service this coming Sunday. No harm in keeping on the right side of the old boy.

It seemed perfectly all right to him, though he didn't much care for all this "Sacred to the memory" rubbish, and he would report back to Sir Logan that he had inspected it for him and found it satisfactory. That should please him.

He walked across the grass towards the gate in the shadow of the graveyard wall. The hedges were beginning to burgeon with their new coat of spring green and the birds were busy in them. The sun sparkled off the loch and soon the tourists would begin to gather. . . .

He had almost reached the gate when he became aware of voices from the road on the other side of the wall and some inborn instinct made him stop to listen to what was being said. Strachan was nothing if not a picker-up of unconsidered trifles.

". . . just yesterday. From Montreal," one voice was saying.

"She's well, is she?" asked the second voice which he recognised as being that of Donald Lachlan, and that determined him to stay quietly where he was.

"Aye, fine, man, fine. She tells me she's getting married again. To some big Canadian lumberjack."

"Well, I just hope he's a better man to her than Roddy ever was," said Donald.

"Oh, he'll be that all right. Linda's not the one to be bitten twice in the same way."

"Aye. It would be a sad thing if she found herself caught up with another one like Roddy. Poor lass. So she'll be settling in Canada then?"

"It looks like it."

"Well, she's wise. I was aye feart she'd take it into her head to come back again in spite of everything. But she'll be out of trouble there. No one can harm her in Canada — unless it's this lumberjack . . ."

The voices faded as their owners moved further down the road and, reaching the gate, Strachan looked after the two unconscious backs moving away from him. Donald Lachlan, sure enough, and the other was that fellow Campbell, the one who used to be such an athlete in his younger days.

He got into the Land Rover and drove thoughtfully back to the Big House. He had found the conversation intriguing. . . .

He reported to Sir Logan about the headstone and on the day's events. The old boy wasn't really interested. Hadn't been since the old biddy had died, really. Seemed to have taken it out of him. Lost a lot of spunk and sparkle these last ten months or so.

He was about to leave Sir Logan in the morning-room when he suddenly stopped.

"Oh, Sir Logan, maybe you can help," he said. "Do you mind if I ask you if the names Linda and Roddy mean anything to you?"

Sir Logan looked at him curiously.

"Yes, they do," he said. "Why do you ask?"

"I just heard them mentioned this afternoon."

Sir Logan turned away and looked out of the window.

"Tragic business," he said. "The McBains. He was a brute, Used to beat her, I understand. He drowned in the loch about ten years ago. His body was never found. Good riddance. She was a pretty little thing. Lovely creature. Deserved a good deal better, dammit. Understand she's in foreign parts."

"Canada, I believe."

"Is that a fact? Well, well. Poor little Linda . . ."

Sir Logan fell into a brown study and Strachan quietly left the morning-room and closed the door behind him.

"No one can harm her there," Lachlan had said. That made sense, if her husband had been a brute. But there was something he'd said just before that about hoping she wouldn't come back "in spite of everything". . . . That was an odd phrase to use. . . .

3

She'd tried to listen at the bedroom door, but either the wood
was too thick or they were speaking in voices too low for her to
hear. Maggie could understand her father speaking low,
because he'd never done anything else in her experience and
recently his voice had become even weaker. It had started at
Lady Peddie's funeral when he'd insisted on standing bare-
headed while the coffin was lowered into the family grave. But
Sir Logan wasn't the man to keep his voice down.

She sat in the living-room, wondering what it was they were
talking about. What was this extraordinary interest Sir Logan
took in her father? Had it anything to do with her? Logic told
her no, but she found it hard to accept.

Supposing, she thought, letting her mind run riot, supposing
Sir Logan and her mother had had an affair? It was possible. Sir
Logan was rumoured to have had affairs with more than one of
the women in the village. That Linda McBain, for instance.
Maybe there was something in Roddy McBain's contention
that it was Sir Logan's child she was carrying. Everyone said
no, that Linda was faithful to that big sadistic brute, but you
never knew . . . and supposing her mother and Sir Logan had
produced *her*? Of course, she had to admit that she could never
understand, when she'd read stories in which that sort of thing
happened, how anyone could be quite sure who the father of
the child was. Perhaps she was completely legal, but maybe Sir
Logan didn't think so, maybe his conscience told him that she
could be his child. . . .

But no, again cold logic took over from the romanticised
idea. If that were so it would be herself Sir Logan lavished his
attention on, not her father. Unless his conscience drove him to
help her father, never admitting to him that *he* was the father,
trying to make reparation for the wrong he had done Graham
Ferguson's wife . . .?

She shrugged the thought away. It was too complicated and
it didn't say very much for her own mother. She remembered
her as a rather plain woman without much personality and with

little to say for herself, but she also remembered that her father and she had been very contented in their own quiet, undemonstrative way.

No, maybe it was simply that they still found things to talk about from the old days, the days in the trenches when so many of their colleagues and friends had been lost. Maybe as you got older clinging to the past like that became more important.

And Sir Logan's visits pleased her father, there was no doubt of that. She had watched the old boy sinking ever since that chill he'd caught at the funeral, his lungs labouring, fighting harder for breath every day, growing weaker and weaker so that now he could only get out of bed for a couple of hours in the afternoon and her work was made that much harder and more time-consuming. He seemed stronger after the visits. More at peace with the world and himself.

And he kept saying that she didn't need to worry. That Sir Logan would see her right. . . .

Why . . .?

4

Hector looked out of the potting shed window at the bedraggled garden. The rain was falling in the puddles along the edge of the flower beds and the grass was saturated. It looked very depressing, but he was not altogether unhappy about it.

He was not a keen gardener at all, and this continuous rain which had gone on for almost the whole of June was an excuse not to have to do anything in the way of horticulture. But it did give him a reason for spending a large part of the day in the potting shed where he could, in fact, potter. He didn't need to do anything constructive in here. He could just sit in the rickety old wooden chair and be at peace and think. . . .

He would have to go in soon, of course, and no doubt Mary would call him from the back door. . . .

Almost as though she had read his mind he heard the back

door open and his heart jumped guiltily, as it always did when she interrupted him thinking disloyal thoughts.

"Hector! Lizzie's here!"

"Coming, dear," he called back and with a sigh of reluctance he got up, shrugged deeper into the old mackintosh he wore, and stepped out of the potting shed. He closed the door and hurried up the path to the back door, shoulders hunched against the rain.

"Slippers, Hector," said Mary as soon as he appeared.

"Yes, dear," he said, stopping on the mat to take his boots off.

"The door, Hector."

"Yes, dear, but in order to close it I shall have to step off the mat on to your clean floor. I haven't got my boots off yet —"

"Well, hurry up, then, and don't stand there chattering. Are we to be left in a draught all afternoon?"

"No, dear. Good afternoon, Lizzie."

"Hello, Hector. How are you?"

"I'm really very well, thank you," he said and left it at that. He was permanently hungry and permanently uncomfortable and often cold, but in spite of that he realised that he didn't feel any different from how he had felt before he got married. Sometimes, in view of that, he wondered why he had done it.

A little later, with his mackintosh hanging on the back door and his boots laid on a piece of newspaper under the sink and wearing his slippers, he found himself with Lizzie and Mary in the living-room which Mary insisted in calling the lounge, and Mary was pouring very weak tea into the best china cups which were only used to show off to Lizzie when she came on her weekly visit.

"And what are you giving the minister for his tea this evening, Lizzie?" demanded Mary.

Lizzie seemed to shrink back in her seat as she usually did when that question was asked.

"Well, he said he felt partial to a steak and kidney pie —"

"No, Lizzie, that will not do at all. Pastry is the last thing you should give him. It's very fattening and full of chosteratol —"

"Of what?"

"Chosteratol. It's a chemical substance which is very very bad for you. I never give my dear Hector *anything* which contains chosteratol . . ."

Hector sat sipping tea quietly and unobtrusively, watching Lizzie getting more and more confused and nervous as Mary chastised her, feeling sorry for her, but slightly relieved because for an hour or so during Lizzie's visit there was no searchlight turned on him, no reminder of his own inadequacies.

He had developed a sort of skin which allowed him to pay little attention to what Mary said, but he did sometimes worry about Lizzie who seemed unable to develop such a skin, and he wondered with some degree of concern how long Lizzie would be able to stand it.

5

As he drove slowly down the track from the road towards the croft house he could see Lachlan bending over the bonnet of the tractor making some kind of adjustment.

Damn the man, he was stubborn. He'd lost the lease to Smith through that stubbornness. He'd told Smith that he would have had Lachlan out by the end of the previous year, but Lachlan had refused to go. And he'd managed to speak to Sir Logan which made it more difficult to put any further pressure on him.

Now Smith had found a croft on an estate somewhere in Sutherland and was no doubt writing reams of epic poetry up there and plaguing the editor of *The Scotsman* with it and thoroughly enjoying himself.

But it had become something of a personal vendetta now to get Lachlan out, even though Smith was no longer in the background to take over the croft and pay a much larger rent for it than he could ever have forced out of Lachlan. But there would be others like Smith. Plenty of others . . .

The croft house still looked neat and in good repair, he thought as he drew the Land Rover to a halt under the tree, but there were satisfactory tell-tale signs. It needed a coat of paint. And Lachlan was obviously having trouble with the tractor.

"Well, Lachlan, how are things with you?" he asked cheerfully as he climbed out of the Land Rover.

Lachlan continued to fiddle around inside the tractor's guts for a moment before withdrawing his head and spitting very deliberately in Strachan's direction.

"Fine," he said.

"Good, good. Just passing and thought I'd look in and see how you all were."

He chatted on about the weather, about the coming crops, about this year's lambs and the prices they had fetched, and he sensed Lachlan getting more and more irritated, wondering what he had really come here for.

"Well, must get on," he said, and turned for the Land Rover. "Oh, one thing, Lachlan," he said suddenly. "Tell me about the McBains."

He turned back quickly and caught the fleeting glimpse he had been hoping for in Lachlan's face. Guilt.

Now, he didn't know what Lachlan was guilty of, and he didn't really care. The McBains meant nothing to him and neither did Lachlan. Lachlan could have bumped both of them off and it wouldn't have worried him. The point was there was guilt, and he knew it and Lachlan knew he knew it and now he had a stranglehold on the man.

"What happened to them?" he asked.

"It was ten years ago," said Lachlan carefully.

"I know that."

"And it was nothing to do with you."

"True. True." He stood smiling at Lachlan for a moment and then turned again to the Land Rover. "Well, well. I suppose it doesn't matter. Oh, by the way, Lachlan. That offer's still open, you know. Any time you decide you'd like a job in Glasgow, you just have to say. All right?"

He started the engine and swung the Land Rover round towards the track again. As he went he saw Lachlan in the driving mirror, standing beside the tractor, staring after him.

6

The row was taking place in undertones so that the rest of the house didn't hear it.

"But I've got her enrolled for St Serf's," Peter said.

He was pacing up and down between the bed and the wardrobe, his face white with anger. Elizabeth sat on the dressing stool, watching him in the mirror.

"Then you'll just have to unroll her again," she said. "You never said anything about that to me."

"Now, that just isn't true, Elizabeth. You know perfectly well we discussed it."

"Oh, we discussed it all right, but we didn't reach any kind of agreement. It strikes me you've been pretty high-handed about this, Peter."

"And you know why that is. You're hardly ever at home now to discuss anything. I find I have to make more and more decisions on my own."

"There's always a telephone."

"There are certain things you can't decide over the telephone. Elizabeth, it's got to stop!"

Elizabeth nodded sadly to herself.

"We certainly can't go on like this," she agreed.

"I will not have any daughter of mine going to the village school in Glendarroch," he said.

"You know, for someone who is always accusing me of being too aristocratic, your own ideas seem strangely upper class."

"You're evading the issue."

"No, I'm not. I just wonder whether your objection to the Glendarroch primary is not because it's a local authority primary, but because it's in Glendarroch. I went to the Glendarroch primary for a couple of years before my parents sent me to St Leonard's, you know. It meant that I had the chance to mix with the local people whom I grew up with, it helped me to understand their lives and their problems in a way I could never have done if I'd lived here in an ivory tower and got sent away to a public school right from the beginning. I want Fiona to have that same chance."

"Her home is in Edinburgh, not here."

"Now, there you've put your finger on the nub of the matter. Where *is* her home? That's something we've never decided."

"Well, *you* seem to have decided. You keep her here against her will —"

"Oh, come off it, Peter! Against her will? The trouble is you've never been in Glendarroch long enough to see how happy she is here compared with Edinburgh."

"I can't see anything wrong with St Serf's and then St George's for her. That's reasonable, she'll be at home, whether you agree that it is home or not, and we needn't pursue this totally unrealistic idea of sending her to St Leonard's. How on earth are we going to afford the boarding fees, for heaven's sake? I'm only a lawyer, not a multi-millionaire."

"I'm sure Dad would help —"

"No! She's our daughter and she's our responsibility. Not your father's."

He stopped suddenly behind her and looked at her in the mirror. She could see that he was building up to some major crisis.

"Elizabeth, I don't often issue orders. I try to let you live your own life as much as possible, but don't you see? This won't do. Since your mother died you've spent almost all your time here. It's not good enough. Tomorrow I am going back to Edinburgh. You and Fiona will come with me. And we will make the final arrangements there for her future education."

"I'm sorry, Peter. I can't."

"I insist."

"Insist away. I shall not be coming."

"Why not, for God's sake?"

"Father needs me here. There is a great deal to do."

He stood breathing heavily for a moment and then turned abruptly and left the bedroom, slamming the door loudly behind him. After the quiet of the quarrel the sound was like a gunshot in its suddenness.

She sat staring at her reflection again, without seeing it. She had won that particular skirmish but the thought gave her no pleasure. What about the war?

Part of what he said was right. They couldn't go on like this. And if she was completely honest with herself, her father didn't need her here. There wasn't really anything important to keep her in Glendarroch. There was no reason why she and Fiona shouldn't go back to Edinburgh with him tomorrow.

But she wasn't going to do it.

7

"Shouldn't he be in hospital, Doctor?" whispered Maggie.

Wallace shrugged.

"There's nothing more they could do for him in hospital," he said. "His lungs are simply giving up, Maggie. And this is his home. I think he's happier, don't you?"

She had to agree to that, and they moved closer to the bed where Graham lay, his breathing thick and noisy, his chest working painfully with the effort. The clock in the hall struck two.

Maggie blinked back tears. What was she crying for? she asked herself impatiently. He'd been nothing but trouble, first to her mother and then to herself, all his life. The trouble wasn't of his making, of course, but it had been trouble nevertheless. That damned war and that foul gas. And it was he who'd had to live with the effects of it all these years. But he was all she had left and now he was going and she felt loneliness gathering in the shadows around her.

Poor old sod . . .

The bell rang briefly, and she went to answer it.

Sir Logan stood in the soft summer darkness outside. He must have walked, for there was no car on the road beyond the gate.

"Maggie, I got your message," he said in a whisper. "How is he?"

"Going, Sir Logan, so Dr Wallace says."

She closed the door quietly behind him and then led the way

to the room at the back where her father slept now. It faced the garden and the loch beyond and it saved him climbing the stairs. He could lie there, as he had done earlier that day, looking out over the water which sparkled in the August sunlight, the water on which he had spent so much of his life, driving that ferry to and from Auchtarne, and there had been a strange peace in his eyes. He knew what was coming and he accepted the inevitable, almost welcomed it.

Sir Logan followed her into the room. She saw him nod briefly to Dr Wallace and then he crossed to the bedside and knelt painfully on the floor. She put a chair beside him but he pushed it away impatiently.

"Ferguson?" he said gruffly and for the first time for over an hour her father responded. It was as if the C.O. had called for him and he answered automatically.

"Sir," he said, though it wasn't easy to make out the word. He was very weak now.

"How is it with you, old friend?" asked Sir Logan.

"Fine, sir. No problem. Cushy billet here, sir . . ."

"Don't try to talk, Graham, man."

Sir Logan grasped one of her father's hands which lay on the eiderdown and held it tightly in both of his.

Maggie stood and watched, an unaccustomed pain in her throat.

They stayed like that, the two of them, silent, without moving, for nearly half an hour and then Maggie became aware of a change in the breathing. Dr Wallace stepped forward to the other side of the bed. Without being told she knew that this was the end.

The breathing seemed to grow more stertorous and less natural. Her father's eyes were open, staring at Sir Logan, not at her at all and she felt a pang of jealousy, but only for a moment. Sir Logan still held her father's hand and she had the curious impression that Sir Logan was drawing strength from him, not he from Sir Logan, and that a conversation was taking place, though her father was far past speech.

And then the breathing stopped quite suddenly and gently and the room was quiet for the first time.

She saw Dr Wallace feeling his pulse and after a moment he shook his head at Sir Logan and came towards her.

"He's gone," he said briefly. "I'm sorry, Maggie."

"He didn't suffer, did he?"

Wallace shook his head sympathetically.

"No more than he has suffered for the last fifty years."

She hardly heard him. She was watching Sir Logan. He still knelt there clasping the dead hand in his and she was astonished to see tears pouring down his cheeks. His shoulders were shaking with sobs.

That, she thought irrelevantly, is the totally wrong reaction if Sir Logan is my father.

8

"What are you doing back so soon?" asked Grace. "I haven't even got the breakfast dishes washed yet."

"I forgot my cromach," said Dougal, taking it from the stand at the door.

"You'd forget your head if it wasn't screwed on," said Grace.

"Actually, I didn't forget it, Mother. Or at least I did, but I forgot it on purpose."

"What are you havering about?"

"I told Father I'd catch up with him. I wanted a word with you. While he wasn't here. It's not easy to get you alone . . ."

She sat down at the kitchen table, pretty certain she knew what Dougal was going to say and wishing he wasn't going to say it, because if he did she would be forced to admit that what she had been dreading for weeks might be true, that it wasn't just her imagination, but that someone else had noticed it too.

"My father," said Dougal. "Is he all right, do you think?"

"Why shouldn't he be?" asked Grace. She *had* been right . . .

"It's just that — well — one or two things. He's slowing down on the hill."

"He's not getting any younger."

"Oh, I know that. And I wouldn't expect him to go on at the

speed he used to. My goodness, Mother, till a month or so ago I couldn't keep up with him. But I can now."

"You're getting faster on the hill yourself, then."

"I know that too. But it's more than that. And his breathing's not too good. He has to stop whiles to gather his strength."

"Have you said anything to him?"

"No. I wouldn't dare. He'd probably scalp me."

"Aye, and it might have the effect of making him try harder. He's a thrawn devil, just like yourself."

"You've noticed, then?"

She nodded reluctantly.

"Aye, I've noticed," she said. "But I haven't said anything either. I was thinking of trying to get word to Dr Wallace, ask him to drop in just in passing, you know, but your father would smell a rat. He's no fool."

"He's not indeed. Is there anything we can do, do you think?"

"I can't think of anything, Dougal, and that's the truth. The only thing is for you to keep an eye on him when you're out with him, make sure he doesn't do too much and get into any trouble."

"All right. I — I'm sorry," he said awkwardly as he got up and headed for the door.

"Dougal."

"Aye?"

"Thank you for telling me. I'd wondered, but I couldn't be sure if it wasn't me imagining things."

Dougal shook his head.

"You're not imagining things." He looked at her helplessly. "The spring's gone from his step, Mother."

"Aye," she said. "And the life from his body."

Dougal turned to go again.

"Dougal."

"Aye?"

"This time you *have* forgotten it," she said, handing him the cromach which he had left propped against the table.

After he'd gone she sat for a long time, thinking. So it was true. And she wondered what the trouble was. She knew Donald was worried by Strachan, that oily factor, but all the crofters were worried by him. And it wasn't just that which was the matter with him, though the worry wouldn't help, of course.

She clasped her hands on the table, and bowed her head.

Oh, God, she thought. Let him be all right.

9

The first snow of the winter had speckled the Big House gardens with white and the light was curiously bright and shadowless in the morning-room as Mrs Cunningham showed Maggie in.

"I'll leave you with him, Maggie," she said. "There are a lot of things to get ready for the New Year Ball. It's Maggie Ferguson, Father," she called and closed the door behind her. Sir Logan rose from his chair at the fire.

"Damned winter again, eh, Maggie?" he said. "Come and sit down, my dear. You must be cold."

He drew a chair in to the fire for her and she wondered what was coming. Some kind of confession, maybe? *"Maggie, I've decided to tell you. You're my daughter. Here's fifty thousand pounds."* No. It wouldn't be quite as dramatic as that. No such luck.

"How are things with you, Maggie? Making out all right?" he asked as he settled back into his own chair.

"Aye, fine, Sir Logan, thank you," she said, shifting a little uncomfortably. Sitting on the other side of the fireplace from the laird seemed all wrong, somehow.

"Bus behaving itself?"

"Very well. It doesn't like the cold first thing in the morning, though."

"Do any of us? Now, look here, Maggie, I want to ask you a rather personal question."

Here it comes, she thought.

"Did your father have any insurance?"

She blinked. That wasn't the question she had expected.

"No," she said. "With his lungs the premium would have been so high we couldn't have afforded it."

He nodded thoughtfully.

"Suddenly struck me, that, the other day," he said. "Dammit, I should have thought of it before. Getting old, Maggie, that's the trouble. Probably damned lucky I thought of it at all. Well, look here, we can't have that. I daresay you'll be finding it difficult to make ends meet, eh?"

"Well, I miss his pension, aye, Sir Logan."

"Exactly. Pension. That's the word. Well, listen to me, I'm going to pay you a pension. Backdated to the time he died. Understand?"

"But — but —"

"No buts. And you don't need to tell anyone about it. Better not, otherwise the tax man may get on to it, know what I mean? It's coming out of my own pocket, Maggie. Not out of the estate books. So you'll get it every week so long as I live. How's that?"

She didn't know what to say. She had never heard of anything so generous before. Sir Logan had never had a name for meanness, but this seemed unusual, to say the least.

"Well, thank you, Sir Logan. It'll make a big difference. But I don't see why you should—"

"Just let me do it, Maggie. In memory of a great man, and a very good friend. All right?"

She nodded, as the same old question rose in her mind once more. Was he doing this because he felt some kind of responsibility for her? Might she in fact be a half-sister to Elizabeth Cunningham, that tall, elegant, well-dressed woman who had shown her in here a few minutes ago? Her mind boggled at the thought, and she remembered what Sir Logan had just said. No. It was nothing to do with her. He was doing this because of her father, and again came that endless, nagging question. *Why . . .?*

10

Jack Campbell stepped on to the bus at Auchtarne Station and Maggie looked up from the driver's seat where she was busy with a thermos flask and a small bottle of milk.

"Back again," she said as if he'd just gone away that morning.

"That's right, Maggie. Home is the sailor. For three months."

She grunted, took his fare and then turned her attention to pouring herself a cup of tea. He grinned, walked down the gangway, slung his kitbag on to the overhead rack and sat down.

It was blowing a March gale out there and some other passengers got on in ones and twos. Just as Maggie screwed the cup on to the top of the thermos again and prepared herself to start the bus, a figure approached from the street beyond the yard and climbed on, paid her his fare and came down the gangway towards him.

"Hallo, Donald," he said.

Donald Lachlan stared at him and then smiled and held out his hand.

"Well, well, Jack Campbell," he said. "So this is you home on leave, is it?"

He sat down beside him as Maggie swung the bus out of the station yard and on to the road to Glendarroch.

"Yes. Three months of freedom."

"Good voyage?"

"A long one. Panama, Valparaiso, Auckland, Fremantle . . ."

"Far away places, eh? It sounds fine."

"It *sounds* it. It's still good to be home, though. How are the old folk, have you heard?"

"I don't see much of them, being stuck up at Ardvain, but I think they're fine, aye."

"And what brings you to Auchtarne? It's not like you to be so far from home."

He detected a slight reserve in Donald's manner.

"Och, I've just been to the doctor."

"Oh? Nothing serious, I hope?"

"No, no. Just a wee check-up. Don't say anything, Jack. Grace doesn't know I've been. I'm not wanting her worried, you ken."

"I'll never let dab," said Jack, glancing at him sideways. Now that they were clear of the buildings and out on the open road the light was clearer in the bus and he could see that Donald Lachlan didn't look good. He was a bad colour for one thing, he who had always seemed so red-cheeked from exposure on the hill.

"It's funny I should meet you today," said Donald, "because I was going to look your father up when we got to Glendarroch before I set off up to Ardvain."

"Then why don't you?"

"Well, I don't want to intrude if this is you just getting home."

"Don't be daft, man. I come home so often it's just like getting back from the office."

"Well, then . . . Do you remember Roddy McBain?"

"Roddy McBain? Him that was drowned in the loch? Aye, I remember him. Why?"

"I just want to have a word with your father about him," said Donald.

When the bus reached Glendarroch they walked together along the road to the Campbells' cottage. His father and mother were waiting at the door, having heard the bus pass, and Donald let him go ahead to greet them.

Coming home was always a pleasure, to see the old folks just as they always had been, the hills round him, and the smoke of the cottage chimneys and the Big House presiding over everything like some benevolent grandfather. . . . Aye, you could keep your big international seaports. It was Glendarroch that mattered.

Later, in the living-room, he listened in growing astonishment as his father and Donald discussed Roddy McBain. It seemed he hadn't drowned in the loch after all. Linda had killed him when he had attacked her in a drunken fury, and his father and Donald and Sorry Watson had helped her on a night wilder than this to bury the body and take his boat out on the loch so that it would be found floating empty the next morning and it would be assumed that he had drowned. Poor Linda . . . She'd lost the child she was carrying. He remembered her. A beautiful, gentle girl, full of love and life. . . .

"You're accessories to murder," he said unbelievingly when his father and Donald had between them told him the whole story.

"Just that," said Jock. "And I'd do it again in those circumstances."

"Your father's right, Jack," said Donald. "I would too. To save Linda. But now we've got trouble. And this is what I wanted to see you about, Jock. I'm glad Jack knows, because he's a good lad and will help us with the problem. Strachan's got a whiff of the story."

"Strachan? The factor?"

"Him."

"What does he know?" asked Jock.

"Not much, but he's a sleekit devil. I wouldn't put it past him to find our more. And he's a man that's dangerous with knowledge."

"He's a shilpit wee craitur," said Jack thoughtfully. He'd met the factor on his last leave and hadn't liked him. And there was something about the man which stirred his memory, though he couldn't think why. He'd seen the face before somewhere . . .

"What's that got to do with it?" asked his father, and he brought his mind back to the present problem.

"I'll see him, if you like," he said. "Tell him if he cheeps one word I'll mangle him."

Donald clicked his tongue and his father shook his head.

"Don't be daft, laddie," he said. "Do you not see? That'll just prove to the man that there's something in whatever it is he's picked up. No. We'll just have to think of something else."

11

It was over a year since he had started this surreptitious travelling and for the first time he was cycling home with a feeling of something like contentment in him.

That was very curious in view of what had just taken place.

The weather was unseasonably mild and benevolent, the stars shining close and friendly in an almost clear sky. As he rode through the April night his thoughts were, as always, of Isabel, but tonight it was not as she was now, how she would be when he got home, asleep in their room with Jimmy in his cot beside her. It was as she was before. . . .

He could not remember a time when she had not been part of his life. She had always been there. He remembered carrying her books home from school for her. They must have been in Primary One then. After that there had been the ferry to Auchtarne every day with old Graham Ferguson in charge. In those days they hadn't even had to wear lifejackets. Maybe that was a symbol of the ease and freedom of life then. What he did remember very clearly was coming back on the ferry one winter day. It had been calm but bitterly cold. The snow-covered mountains round the loch were like a calendar photograph, lovely to look at but hostile and remote. Isabel had shivered and, greatly daring, for the first time he had put an arm round her to try to protect her from the cold. There had been physical contact before, of course, but this was something new, strange and perhaps a little frightening in its difference. She had snuggled into him without a giggle or a protest as if it was the most natural thing to do. It was the other kids who had giggled but he didn't care about them. They didn't count. But Graham Ferguson had looked at them and smiled gently and then looked away to make sure the boat was heading in the right direction, studiously leaving them to themselves. He supposed they'd both been about fourteen at the time.

Perhaps it was then that they had each known they were meant for each other, and yet it had been tacitly acknowledged long before that, not only by themselves but by everyone they knew. That day on the ferry had been some kind of symbolic acknowledgement of the unspoken fact, and from then on nothing further needed to be said, until one day when they were walking down to the ferry early one summer morning. It must have been their last year at school, and she'd stopped to tie a shoelace. He looked at her kneeling there at the side of the path, her hair covering her face as she bent to the task, and he'd suddenly said out of the blue:

"I love you."

She hadn't said anything, just finished tying her lace. Then she'd straightened up and taken his hand and squeezed it gently and that had been quite enough. They hadn't even kissed. They'd walked on to the ferry in a happy daze.

And other memories crowded in on him, of birthday parties, of Christmases and of days of doing homework together, either in his parents' or her parents' living-room, days on the hills during the holidays when the sun was warmer and the grass greener and the sky bluer than it ever seemed now and it never seemed to rain. Isabel laughing and happy, caring and tender. An integral part of his life. Without her he was only half a being. Isabel, Isabel, Isabel . . .

He freewheeled down the village street, the headlight bouncing gently along the road ahead of him, and dismounted at the old garage, wheeled the bike across the cracked and broken paving of the yard where the weeds were sprouting now in riotous confusion, skirted the dangerous stump of the old petrol pump and pulled open the door. He padlocked the bike as usual to the leg of the bench inside and then went out, pulled the door to and padlocked it with the old padlock he'd found in his toolbox at home. It was rusty on the outside, though he'd oiled the inside so that it made no noise and it matched the bolt on the garage, so probably no one would have noticed that the door which for years had been only pulled to was now closed and made fast.

He wondered if he would be using it again, whether there was any point in keeping the bicycle, because now he had no further need for it.

That night Avril had roused him to a peak of physical desire and then suddenly withdrawn from him.

"Listen, pet, what about this divorce?" she'd said.

He'd shaken his head and she'd climbed out of bed and begun to dress.

"Then that's it, isn't it, pet? You just been usin' me, haven't you? Well, it won't do. I know I'm not an angel, but I do have my pride."

He'd lain there looking at her, feeling nothing now that the animal instinct had been frustrated. In a way he could understand her attitude. He couldn't pay her vast sums of money for her services, because he didn't have them. But she had had trinkets and jewellery and bits of clothing, and she'd had her own obvious and insatiable appetite which he supposed he'd been able to satisfy. She was right to say he'd been using her. That was exactly what he had been doing and he was to blame for that. But he sometimes wondered how many other people were using her at the same time. He had become pretty sure that her facile use of unused hotel rooms, sheets and towels was through frequent practice.

Give up Isabel for this? He'd actually laughed at the thought.

She'd thrown a tantrum then, a quiet one, because they both knew that two of the rooms along this corridor were occupied, but she'd made it quite clear that unless he was prepared to do the right thing by her she was going to withdraw her services. Maybe she knew that she'd got as much out of him in the way of worldly goods as she could and that there was no point in going on any longer. Or maybe she had better prospects elsewhere.

In a way it had been a relief. He was quit of her, quit of the subterfuge and the sordid meetings. It was a relief to feel clean again.

Though he didn't think that life was going to get any easier.

He pocketed the padlock key and turned for home.

12

The pain came when he was halfway up the hill. Dougal was ahead of him with Bess, and he had been trying to keep up with them, which was something he did with increasing difficulty now.

He stopped and the pain receded. Just a twinge, he thought, rubbing his shoulder. Maybe something I ate at breakfast which didn't agree with me.

Dougal stopped and looked back and Donald pretended simply to be looking out at the loch and the hills on either side as though he had never seen them before.

"You all right, Dad?"

He nodded.

"Aye, of course," he said. "That's bonny, isn't it? Maybe we should stop and look at the view more often than we do."

Dougal came back towards him, and Donald could see the worry in his eyes.

"Aye, it is," he agreed, but without looking at the view at all. "Do you think maybe we should go home . . .?"

"No, no, of course not. Tell you what. Why don't you give Bess a bit of exercise, eh? See how she handles those yowes there."

Dougal looked surprised but after a moment he nodded and moved away, whistling to Bess to join him.

Donald leant against a stone wall, watching as Dougal put Bess through her paces. It wasn't necessary. Bess was a good dog with sheep and Dougal handled her well. But standing watching meant that he didn't have to face the hill again for a while, gave him a chance to take a breather and let the pain diminish. In five or ten minutes he felt better.

He knew he hadn't fooled Dougal. Dougal knew there was something wrong. Grace knew it too, and he felt a sudden sense of panic which nearly set the pain going again, but he forced it down. Panic wasn't going to help.

And there was nothing to panic about. Dr Wallace had suggested he should give up the croft, maybe retire and take things easy, but he had vehemently rejected the idea because at the back of his mind was the thought that that was what Strachan wanted and he wasn't going to give in to *him*. Wallace had looked worried and told him that his heart wasn't in the best of condition. But how could he take it easy? Quite apart from Strachan the croft and the sheep were his life. He had no wish to become a vegetable, sitting in front of the fire all day, getting in Grace's way, watching Dougal doing the work.

Dougal had allowed Bess to go too wide rounding the yowes into a corner and a couple of them had escaped. But he couldn't blame him. Dougal wasn't watching Bess. He was watching him. He was pretending not to, but Dougal's attempts at subtlety had never been very good and Donald knew what was going through his mind.

Oh, well. If it happened it happened and at least he had the comfort of knowing that the croft would be in good hands when Dougal eventually took it over.

That is, if they still had it and Strachan didn't manage to force them out. . . .

13

"Hello, Maggie."

She nearly spilt the thermos into her lap. She'd been concentrating on pouring tea from it into the cup as she sat waiting for the passengers from the Glasgow train to make their way from the platform to the bus, and she'd heard someone getting on, but hadn't bothered to look and see who it was.

"Sorry Watson, look what you've made me do," she said.

"You haven't spilt it, have you, Maggie?"

"No, but I very nearly did."

"I'm sorry —"

"And never a word from you."

"I didn't think you'd want me to write."

"I didn't."

"Well, then—"

"But it would have been a courtesy," she snapped, screwing

the thermos together again as another group of passengers came out of the booking hall and made their way to the bus. "Now for goodness sake go and sit down and stop making a nuisance of yourself."

He paid his fare and blinked and smiled at her in that stupid, shy way he had and then carried the battered old suitcase to the back and sat down where no one would see him.

A little later she started the engine and drove the bus out of the station yard and on to the road to Glendarroch, all the time very conscious of his eyes boring into the back of her neck. It was really very disconcerting.

At Glendarroch she drew to a halt opposite the path which led to the store and watched as the passengers got off, counting them as they did so. He wasn't amongst them. She turned in her seat and he was still sitting at the back, looking embarrassed.

"Well, are you getting off or not?" she asked.

"Yes, of course, Maggie."

He got hastily to his feet, grabbed the suitcase and came down the gangway towards her. When he reached her he took off his cap and stood in front of her, twisting it in his hands.

"I was sorry about your father, Maggie," he said.

"Who?" she asked sarcastically. "Oh, him. I'd forgotten. After all it's nearly two years since he died. Fancy you remembering. You didn't write about that either."

"Are you — I mean, how are you getting on now?"

"You mean, have I got enough money?"

"I was wondering —"

"Well, you can stop wondering, and there's no need for you to ask me to marry you again, because the answer's still no."

"Oh."

"I'm doing fine. The bus is covering its costs and I've got a grand wee pension comes in every month from Sir Logan —"

"From Sir Logan?"

"Has Shetland made you deaf? Sir Logan."

"Why is he paying you a pension?"

"That's none of your business."

"I know, Maggie. I'm sorry. I just wondered why he would do a thing like that."

"Sorry Watson, I'll thank you to keep your long nose out of my affairs, do you hear me?" she said with more indignation than she had meant, because she had been wondering the same thing herself for long enough.

She watched as he climbed off the bus and hefted that awful old suitcase of his and set off along the road, feeling very angry because he had raised doubts in her which she thought she had managed to submerge.

14

"Look here, Watson, what the devil has it got to do with you?" barked Sir Logan angrily.

Sorry blinked. He'd put it wrong, but it had been difficult to know how best to broach this subject.

"I'm sorry, Sir Logan," he said. "Please. Let me explain."

Sir Logan humphed and growled and then settled back in his chair on the other side of the desk in the window of the morning-room. Sorry sat on the edge of a hard chair in front of him, feeling like a schoolboy facing the headmaster.

"I've just come back from Shetland, Sir Logan," he said.

"Yes. Understood you'd gone and settled there. Very bleak place, Shetland."

"Yes, Sir Logan, it is. But beautiful too. The reason I came back is because I've got the chance to make a bit of money. The smallholding my uncle left me is set right on a part of the shore where one of the big oil companies wants to build a terminal for this oil they're expecting to get out of the North Sea. They've offered me a very good price for it. I think I could hold out for more, but I thought I'd come and see how things were here with Maggie before I made up my mind."

Sir Logan fixed him with a piercing eye.

"Sweet on the girl, are you, Watson?" he asked.

"Yes, Sir Logan. I have been for a long time. She's — well — I think she likes me well enough, although it's not easy to tell from her manner, but she's always said she won't marry me. I think she's got the feeling that she could do better for herself."

"So?"

"Well, I came back hoping that I might persuade her to marry me after all, with this money behind me. But now I find that she's getting a pension from you."

"Ah. Yes. I understand what's worrying you, Watson. Dammit, you want me to stop paying her this pension, is that it?"

"Well, actually, yes, Sir Logan. I mean, I appreciate you doing it and all that, but I do feel it's more my responsibility than yours, if you see what I mean."

"You're wrong there, you know."

"I suppose if you did stop this pension it might look as if between us we were blackmailing her into marrying me and I wouldn't want that. If you could maybe just tell me why you're paying it to her, I might find it easier to understand and perhaps I could — well — plan my strategy accordingly."

Sir Logan turned and stared thoughtfully out of the window for a few minutes.

"Can't give up paying it to her, dammit," he said gruffly.

Sorry was about to ask why but an instinct told him it would be better not to say anything, that Sir Logan was on the brink of telling him anyway.

"It's because of her father, you understand. He was one of the best, Watson, the absolute best." He was silent again, drumming his fingers on the desk in front of him. Then he sighed and seemed to make up his mind. "All right," he said. "I've never told anyone this before, Watson. Not even my wife, bless her. No one knows this now except me. But I think someone else ought to know. For the future. For Ferguson's good name. He was my batman, you know."

Sorry nodded.

"In the first war," he said.

"It was on the Somme. We were up the line. The Boche were up to something but we didn't know what. This was 1918. Getting on for the end, though we didn't know it then, of course. Ferguson and I were out on a recce, just the two of us, and suddenly there it was. This thick, yellow cloud rolling towards us. The Boche had launched a gas attack. Not the chlorine they'd used earlier. Mustard gas. Devilish stuff. And you know what, Watson? I'd left my mask back in the dug-out. My own stupid fault. We knew what it was all right. Ferguson gave me a mask. And I took it. I swear I thought he must be carrying a spare, but he wasn't, and I didn't know that until it was too late. He caught the gas. I didn't. He gave me his mask, you see."

Sorry blinked again and remained quiet, watching the old man's profile as he stared out of the window at the lawns and flower beds beyond, bright in the June sunshine, not seeing them, seeing again that silent yellow cloud as he must have seen it so often through the intervening years.

"It should have been me, coughing and wheezing my way through this last half century. Not Ferguson. You understand now?"

Sorry nodded.

"Conscience money," he said gently and without rancour.

"Absolutely. Tried to look after Ferguson as well as I could all these years. Now it's up to me to look after his daughter."

There was silence for a while. He saw Elizabeth Cunningham cross the lawn with a little girl skipping beside her. He assumed it was her daughter. She looked about seven years old now. Was it as long ago as that . . .?

"So what are you thinking of doing, Watson?" asked Sir Logan.

"I think," said Sorry after a long agonised silence, "it would be better if I went back to Shetland just now. Let you go on salving your conscience."

Sir Logan looked at him and there was gratitude in his eyes.

"You're a very understanding fellow, Watson. I appreciate that. You understand why I'd like to go on helping her so long as I'm here?"

"I understand that, Sir Logan. But afterwards?"

"Ah. Afterwards. That's the crunch, isn't it? I can't ask Elizabeth to carry on paying a pension to salve my conscience, as you put it."

"No. Indeed you can't. Suppose I go back to Shetland. Try to hold out for more money."

"And wait for me to die, you mean?" Sir Logan said harshly.

"Not exactly. Try to make sure that I have more money to offer Maggie than you ever could, Sir Logan. You could go on paying her this pension because it wouldn't matter then, you see. That's what I had in mind."

Sir Logan stared at him and then chuckled suddenly.

"That sounds like a sporting offer, Watson. Good of you to take it that way."

"But I'd better warn you. I've never actually had to do any bargaining in my life. I have the feeling that it's something I shall enjoy and that I'll be good at. So I may be back sooner than you expect."

Sir Logan stood up.

"Good for you, Watson. Let's shake on that." He held out his hand and Sorry took it. Sir Logan held it for a moment and looked directly into his eyes. "You know, I wept salt tears when Ferguson died. But in a way it was a relief. He wasn't there to make me feel guilty any more."

15

Jack Campbell reached the top of the hill and flung himself down with a sigh of pleasure. There was something satisfying about gaining a height. He spent most of his life looking at the flatness of the sea.

He pulled a paper bag out of his pack and unwrapped the sandwiches his mother had made for him that morning. As he ate hungrily he looked at the view below. There was the village, nestling in a bight of the loch, and on the other side he could even see Auchtarne. The hills faded into the distance, blue and purple, the sunlight dappling their slopes and glinting on the surface of the loch where the summer pleasure boats were crawling like ants.

He finished his sandwiches and took out the thermos of coffee. There was a gentle breeze but even at this height it wasn't strong, and the sun blazed down from an almost cloudless sky.

What a magical place, he thought. Wherever his ship might take him it was always a pleasure to come home.

Later he screwed up the paper bag and replaced it carefully in his pack with the thermos, hefted the pack on to his back again and began the downward slope on the opposite side to his ascent.

Ardvain crept into view round a shoulder of the hill and then the track which wound up to it. He could see the crofts dotted here and there in the hollow between the hills. There was greenness down there, covered with the white dots of sheep.

A vehicle was standing on the track and he stopped to look at it. It must be about two miles away, looking like a Dinky toy, but in the crystal clarity of the air he recognised its colour and shape as being one of the estate Land Rovers.

Probably the man Strachan, he thought, and again he felt that nagging sense of impatience because he couldn't place the face. He'd seen it somewhere before. Not here. Somewhere else. If only he could think where it had been he might get it . . .

There didn't seem to be anyone in the Land Rover. He stood and searched the area between it and the foot of the slope he was descending but could see no sign of the man.

About a mile away he made out a figure moving, but he recognised it through long familiarity as being Donald Lachlan. He turned his steps down that way so that he might intercept him, find out how he was and get news of Grace and Dougal.

A spur of hill cut off his view for about a quarter of an hour as he descended. He joined a tributary of the Darroch which burbled down the hillside through a stand of trees and he was almost at the outer fringe of them when he became aware of voices, carried to him across quite a distance through the clear air.

He couldn't hear what was said but he could sense the anger in one of them, and it was the voice of Donald Lachlan.

He frowned and hurried on a little faster.

The voices got louder but before he could make out words he suddenly heard a stifled cry and an abrupt silence, followed by the other voice which now had a note of urgency in it.

He began to run, not an easy job on so steep a slope, and he found himself breaking his headlong rate of progress with his hands against tree trunks, until he came out at the rim of an open hollow and there at the bottom he spotted the two figures, one sprawled on his back, the other bending over him.

He slid and slithered down the slope. The bending figure heard his approach and looked up.

Strachan.

"Quick!" he called as Jack approached. "I think he's had a heart attack. Get help!"

Jack came up to them and knelt beside Donald. He was very pale, his breath short and shallow, and his face had turned a bit blue.

"You go," he said. "I'll stay here."

"No, you go . . ."

"Do you know anything about first aid?" snapped Jack, taking a chance.

The man shook his head.

"Then run!"

And after a moment's hesitation Strachan hurried away.

Jack wondered what to do. He had no knowledge of first aid himself, but he didn't like the idea of Donald being left alone with Strachan, especially after what he had heard of the difficulties between the two. There was also the suspicion that this might not have been an accident, though there was no sign of a struggle or of injury. He knew enough to feel for a pulse, but it took him a long time and when he found it at last at the side of Donald's neck, it was weak and fluttery.

Kiss of life, he thought, but he didn't really know enough about it.

Donald was unconscious and when he tentatively lifted an eyelid there was no sign of the iris. That, he believed, was a bad sign.

"Hurry. *Hurry*!" he muttered helplessly to himself.

He tried a rough sort of mouth to mouth resuscitation, breathing into Donald's mouth, then pressing his chest downwards, hoping he was doing the right thing.

But it was no use.

Ten minutes later when the mouth to mouth seemed to have had no effect, he felt for the pulse again and this time he couldn't find it.

16

Sir Logan shook hands with Grace and Dougal, trying to find adequate words of comfort for them. She looked pale and sad, he thought. But not shocked. He had the feeling she might have been expecting something like this for some time.

"The croft is yours now, Dougal," he said. "I'm sure you'll manage it as well as your father did."

"I'll try, Sir Logan," said Dougal and he looked as if he wanted to say something else, but Elizabeth was waiting behind him.

"I'll have the lease transferred to your name as soon as possible. Get everything shipshape and above board," he said, moving away to let Elizabeth take his place.

He walked out of the graveyard with his hands behind his back, feeling once again how fragile our hold on life was. You couldn't have imagined anyone with a healthier life than Donald Lachlan. The last subject for a heart attack, you'd have thought. But that had been what it was all right. Because it was a sudden death there had been an autopsy and the result proved beyond doubt that it was what young Wallace called a myocardial infarction. He also said that Donald had consulted him about it some time ago, too . . .

"Good morning, Logan."

He came out of the brown study he had been in.

"Oh. Morning, George."

George Carradine and his son, young George, had attended the funeral too. George was a contemporary. One of the few he felt he could meet on an equal footing. He was also the estate and family lawyer.

"Like a chat with you, if you feel up to it?" said George.

"What the devil do you mean, if I feel up to it? I'm younger than you are, you old fraud."

"Only by three months. Glendarroch House?"

"Of course."

"Fine. Mind if I bring young George with me?"

"Not at all. Outnumber me if you want to, so long as you don't charge me two consultation fees."

George laughed and young George smiled politely and Sir Logan stepped into the car, the door of which Syme was holding open for him, and settled back to wait for Elizabeth.

What now, he wondered?

17

They left the graveyard and walked back towards the store in silence. He'd tried to take her arm, not with any degree of hope of making contact, but purely for the look of the thing to other people, but she had gently and firmly disentangled herself from it.

They nodded and smiled a little as they passed people, each of them acting out the part of the happily married couple, for the graveyard had been well attended. Although Donald Lachlan had not often been seen in Glendarroch he was a popular figure in the village.

Their path took them past the old garage. It looked even more decrepit by daylight and his heart missed a beat as they came in view of the old forecourt with the stump of the single petrol pump which itself had rusted into disuse long ago.

Standing at the door in a bright green low-cut dress and black shoes with what looked like four-inch heels, was Avril Hendry.

He averted his eyes, but not before she'd caught them and had smiled conspiratorially at him.

God, what was she going to do? he asked himself and felt relief as they walked past and she did nothing. Isabel didn't notice her.

He steeled himself not to hurry, to maintain the same pace they had taken since they left the graveyard, and they passed the garage without incident and returned to the shop where Mrs

Woods was looking after Jimmy. Isabel took him from her and began a bright and artificial chatter about how moving the ceremony had been and how much they would all miss Donald.

Brian slipped quietly out.

He hurried back to the garage and found her waiting there.

"I kent you'd not be long," she greeted him.

He gestured her to silence and slipped round the back of the garage where they would be out of sight of the road and the surrounding cottages. He wondered desperately how many people might be watching him at this very moment.

"What did you come here for?" he demanded as soon as she joined him in the little walled courtyard at the back where old Richards used to service cars.

"Thought it was time we had another talk, pet," she said. "About this divorce."

"I've told you before, I'm not looking for a divorce."

"Maybe, pet, but that didn't stop you from lookin' for other things, did it? Okay. You win. If that's the way you want it. No divorce."

For a moment he felt a sense of relief. It was over. . . .

"I'll take a thousand pounds instead," she said.

He stared at her, feeling as if all the breath had been driven out of his body.

"That's crazy," he said when he'd recovered. "Where do you think I could raise a thousand pounds?"

She shrugged uncaring shoulders.

"I'd have thought it was cheap at the price. You see, with a thousand pounds I could afford to go to Glasgow and get rid of it."

For a moment he thought she meant the thousand pounds and then her real meaning sank into his befuddled brain.

"You're — you're —" he stuttered and she nodded.

"Aye," she said. "Go on. Say it. With child. Pregnant. In the puddin' club. Get it?"

"You can't be. We were very careful —"

"Not careful enough, obviously, were you, pet? So I need that thousand pounds. To get you out of trouble."

He stared at her and wondered how he could ever have imagined her attractive.

"And is that all you'll ever want?"

"Don't know what you mean, pet. Oh, blackmail, is that what's worryin' you? Well, once I've got rid of it I haven't got proof any longer, have I? No, pet. It's a one-off payment. For services rendered. Cheap at the price, I'd have thought, all things considered."

He shook his head.

"I haven't got it," he said and a flash of anger surged through him. "And even if I did have it, you wouldn't get it."

"Was that the wife went past with you just now?"

He watched her warily.

"Mousey lookin' thing, isn't she? I wonder how she'd react if she knew just what her lovin' husband's been up to?"

She took a mirror out of her bag and examined her face in it, using her tongue to lick a bit of lipstick off a front tooth.

"Think about it, pet, and let me know. Soon, though, eh? Much longer and it'll be too late for me to do anythin' about it, know what I mean?"

She turned and walked off, looking slightly ridiculous in those high heels which kept turning on the uneven surface of the path round the side of the garage, leaving him standing with his hands clenched tight. The sound of her footsteps tap-tapped into silence.

18

"I simply had no idea."

Sir Logan sat back in his chair at the desk and looked helplessly at the two Carradines. The shock of their revelations hadn't sunk in yet, but he was beginning to feel the first tremors of what it all meant and what it would mean from now on. . . .

"You mean we're bankrupt?" he said, forcing himself to ask the question.

Old George smiled and shook his head.

"Hardly that, Logan. No, no. It's just that things are a lot worse than you evidently knew. I have to say, though, that I don't understand how you didn't."

"I can honestly say I had no idea, George."

"No. I can see that. Strachan should have kept you informed."

"Perhaps he simply wanted to spare me concern. He's a good factor."

"Hm," said George non-committally. "I'd have thought a good factor's job was to keep the owner informed about the financial standing of the estate."

"What can I do?"

George sat back and placed the tips of his fingers together judiciously.

"As I see it you have three alternatives. One, you can sell out while you can and still get a good price for the estate."

"Never!"

Sir Logan sprang to his feet and felt his head swim a little as he did so. He shouldn't have moved so rapidly. As it cleared he found himself looking out at that dear familiar view across the lawns down to the loch and the hills beyond. He knew every blade of grass, every bush and tree, every stone and flower, every knob and hollow in the hills. They were his life, his heritage. Without them he was nothing. All right, without him they would be unchanged, uncaring, and that was depressing and, he felt, a trifle unfair. But the people. They were what mattered. The part of the estate which he couldn't look out of the window at, which he didn't need to see, because he knew they were there, getting on with their daily lives as their fathers and grandfathers and great-grandfathers had done back into the mists of time. They needed him. To abandon them, leave them to the mercy of someone new and unknown. No. It was unthinkable.

"No. Quite unthinkable," he said aloud.

"Then you can develop," said George.

"What do you mean, develop? Holiday camps and pony trekking? Tourist pubs and yacht marinas? I daresay it'll come to that, George, but not in my time, I sincerely hope. And there's one big disadvantage. All that would take capital. And from what you were saying, we haven't got any."

"It could be raised."

Mortgages, loans, repayments, the whole sordid business of finance. It was something he knew nothing about and therefore he shied away from it in fear and distrust. That might be for Elizabeth. And Peter. This could be where Peter might fit into the Glendarroch scheme. His business acumen and his connections in Edinburgh might at least become of some value. If only he could be persuaded to take an interest in it. It had been one of the disappointments of his life that Peter had not been able to fit into the life of Glendarroch, become part of the family which made up the estate.

He grunted non-committally.

"You said three alternatives," he said.

"Thirdly, pull in your horns," said George.

Sir Logan laughed without humour.

"I don't see that as an alternative," he said. "We're going to have to do that anyway."

"And put up the rents again."

"I don't like that —" he began and then took in the last word George had said. "What do you mean *again*?"

George looked at him strangely.

"Didn't you know? Strachan's put them up four times in the last six years," he said.

Sir Logan stared at him, feeling a slight chill in the pit of his stomach.

"No," he said. "I didn't know that."

19

His plan of action was based on two facts.

Firstly, he didn't have a thousand pounds.

Secondly, Isabel must never know anything about this. No one knew better than he how he had been abandoned and ignored by Isabel during the years since they lost their second child. No one knew better than he how Jimmy had been withdrawn from his affections. And at the same time no one knew better than he that it wasn't her fault. It was an accident of fate. Sometime, somehow she would come out of this trauma she was living in and become the same dear Isabel he had known all his life. But if she heard about Avril Hendry that day might be put off for ever.

So his plan was made, and having made it he began to put it into operation, having thought it all out, all the ramifications, all the alternatives, and although some of them he couldn't insure against and although he knew his plan wasn't foolproof he felt that he now knew what was the best thing to do and he couldn't put off doing it any longer.

At midday he rang the Auchtarne Arms from the callbox near the church and asked to speak to Avril Hendry. No personal calls for staff, he was told, but he was prepared for that and said it was an urgent family matter, so after a bit of humphing she was summoned to the telephone.

The sound of her voice didn't affect him at all now. There was no affection left, there wasn't even hatred. She was nothing more than an obstacle to keeping Isabel safe and sane.

"Hullo," she said.

"If you want your thousand pounds you'd better be in Glendarroch this evening."

"Oh, it's you," she said cautiously, and he knew that there was someone listening to her at the other end.

"Same place as last time. Get the four-thirty bus."

"All right."

He knew she'd be off duty till seven-thirty that night, and he put the telephone down without saying another word.

He had no idea how he spent the rest of the day. He wandered outside the village where no one would see him, where he wouldn't have to speak to anyone and have his mind taken away from the rut into which he had prepared it to fall.

He was behind the garage a little after five and he made everything ready. The July day had darkened from a bright morning and now there was a thin drizzle of rain beginning to fall, but he scarcely noticed it. It wasn't at all cold.

At half-past five he heard the familiar tap of heels and she appeared on the path beside the garage, a small red umbrella which he'd given her a year ago held over her carefully coiffeured hair.

"Hallo, pet, what a beast of a day," she said. "Let's get it over with quick, eh? I'll need to get the bus back."

She held out a hand, but he kept his in his pockets.

"I haven't got it," he said.

The smile disappeared from her face as though someone had used a windscreen wiper on it.

"Have you brought me all this way just to tell me that?" she demanded shrilly.

"No. I asked you to come here to ask you to forget the whole thing. Give it up."

"You must be jokin'."

"I'm not, Avril. I'm pleading with you. Please. Give it up."

She stared at him for a long time and he saw the anger and the thwarted greed in her eyes. Then she suddenly threw back her head and laughed. He could see the fillings in her teeth.

"D'you think I'm soft?" she asked. "Come off it, pet. I told you. The money or your wife. That's good, isn't it? She at home just now, is she? Suppose we go and see her? You and me together, eh?"

"Please, Avril —"

"God. Mr Universe, himself," she said, looking him up and down contemptuously. "Let me tell you somethin', pet. You're damn lucky it isn't five thousand I'm asking for. If you'd been any bloody good in bed it would have been . . ."

She began to abuse him, her voice rising. He switched off, not wanting to listen, because it made him angry, but the anger was there already and he couldn't keep it down. He'd pleaded with her, given her her last chance. Tried to help her and she hadn't taken it. Now he knew, finally and irrevocably, that there was only one thing left to be done.

He'd selected the metal pipe before she arrived. It lay on the top of an old oil drum and he picked it up and hit her with it.

She looked at him with an expression of surprise on her face.

"Here, what d'you do that for —?" she asked and stopped

talking in mid-sentence as her eyes, those over-made-up eyes, glazed over.

He hit her again and she whimpered briefly, put up her arms to protect her head, and then began to crumple. Her knees gave and she staggered, losing one of the high-heeled shoes.

A terrible feeling of power came over him, and also of relief.

God, he thought, it's so easy, and he hit her again and again as the drizzle strengthened into a downpour and the blood began to mingle with the puddles forming in the courtyard.

20

Wallace looked up as young George Carradine put his head round the consulting room door.

"Come in, George," he said. "Sit down. The more I see of life and death, the more I realise I don't understand either. Brian Blair. I can't believe it."

Carradine sat down in the chair opposite the desk.

"I'm afraid it's true," he said.

"Are you sure?"

"Well, I've just come from seeing him. He confessed to Sergeant Phimister and Constable Murray and he confessed to me."

"Good God!"

"You've completed the autopsy?" asked Carradine, and Wallace felt himself shudder as he nodded.

"Yes. Hateful job. I wish there was a pathologist within call. Pretty horrendous injuries, George. You don't want details, do you? There wasn't much of the cranium left."

"No, I don't want details. Not at the moment, anyway. Can I ask you a question?"

"Of course."

"Was she pregnant?"

"Pregnant? No."

"Are you sure?"

"George, I am a doctor."

"I know. I'm sorry. But it's important, you see."

"Why?"

"Well, if she wasn't pregnant it means it was blackmail."

"Does that help?"

"I don't know. Possibly not. You see, Brian's not saying anything, apart from the fact that he killed her because she was pregnant. And I've got a feeling he's not going to say anything, even if we put him in the witness box. I don't understand."

He's protecting Isabel, thought Wallace. Of course that's what it is. So he won't say anything at the trial. . . .

Have I the right to tell George about their relationship? No. If Brian wants anything said he will say it himself. But I'd better have a word with Brian, just to be sure. . . .

"So I'm glad to know it was blackmail. Because when it comes to the trial," Carradine was going on, "I'm afraid Brian Blair's going to need all the help he can get."

21

"No, Elizabeth, there is nothing I can do that George Carradine can't do," said Peter. "The case will be heard at the High Court in Glasgow, not in Edinburgh, and Carradine will have all the details at his fingertips, which is more than I have. He's quite capable of instructing counsel without interference by me."

Elizabeth sat back with a sigh. There were children playing in the park again, as there always were when the weather was sunny. It should have provided a feeling of timelessness, but it only made her feel that time was inevitably passing with increasing speed. Each year the children were different. And this year Fiona was one of them. . . .

"It's just that I feel — I feel —" she said and stopped, because she wasn't quite sure what she felt.

"Useless?" Peter finished for her. "I understand that. And I don't like to say it, but you are. There is nothing you can do. It's a legal matter now to be fought out in the courts, though by all accounts there won't be much fighting to be done."

"No, that isn't it at all. I know legally I'm useless. I just feel I should be there."

"In Glendarroch?"

"Yes."

"Why? Brian Blair isn't there. He's in Glasgow now, isn't he?"

"Yes."

"And will remain there till the trial. The focus has shifted to Glasgow and that's where it'll stay. And don't you go thinking that you can do any good. The time for knights in shining armour is long past. There is nothing you can do. I must go. I shall be late."

He kissed her cheek and a moment later she heard the front door of the flat slam shut as he left for the office.

She began to clear the breakfast table, taking the dishes through to the kitchen, her mind not at all on what she was doing.

She knew he was right, admitted the logic of what he said, but that didn't make her feel any different. Brian Blair was one of her people. And that was where she should be. With her own people. Not here.

22

The bleak January light had faded early, soon after two o'clock, and the telephone, when it rang, was a shock, even though they had been waiting for it all day.

Her mother answered it in the shop, and Isabel sat there, feeling the tension mounting in her as it had been mounting for days now, weeks even, and she wondered how much further it could mount before something inside her snapped.

She clutched the arms of her chair so that the loose covers were ridged under her fingers, and she listened to her mother's voice coming from the shop, although she couldn't make out the words. After a moment she heard the ting as the receiver was replaced and a minute later her mother came through into the living-room, her face pale.

"That was Mr Carradine," she said. "It's life."

Isabel said nothing, still gripping the loose covers. She felt herself begin to shake. The shaking, once started, wouldn't stop. It got worse and worse and she felt her teeth clench and bite her tongue and her whole body went rigid.

"Isabel? Are you all right? Isabel!"

Her mother's voice seemed to come from a great distance and the shaking got worse and worse until she felt as if she were being tossed around in some huge cement mixer, her teeth rattling and her bones vibrating. She wished it would stop, but it wouldn't, it just went on and on. She was very vaguely aware of her mother leaving her and she thought she heard her voice shouting some distance away, but who to and what she was saying she couldn't make out, and then everything began to go grey and it got greyer and greyer until it turned to black and she didn't know anything more. . . .

". . . It's all right, Isabel. Everything's fine. Come on, now. You can wake up."

Something was shaking her and for a moment she thought it was a continuation of that awful shaking, but it wasn't. There was a hand on her shoulder and it was that which was doing the shaking, and she opened her eyes and tried to focus. It took some time, but at last she became aware of a face looking down at her, fuzzy and indistinct, but even as she looked it seemed to form more solidly.

Sandy Wallace.

"Sandy . . ." she said, and her voice sounded weak but like her own.

"Yes, it's me. How do you feel?"

"Funny . . ."

"That's natural. You know what's happened, don't you?"

The question brought it all back to her.

"Brian . . ." she said. "They've sent him to prison . . . for life . . ."

"That's right."

She tried to struggle up as though there was something she could do about it, but he pushed her back and she hadn't the strength to resist. He began to talk to her, very slowly and clearly and loudly.

"Listen to me, Isabel. Life doesn't mean life, you know. At the most it's fifteen years. There'll be time off for good conduct. Say ten years. That's something you can live with, isn't it?"

Of course it was. But there were other things which she couldn't live with and as she thought of them, as they began to force their way into her mind she lay back with a groan and began to cry. It was like that awful shaking. Once started she couldn't stop. It got worse and worse. She felt her whole body wracked with the sobs which seemed to be tearing her apart, and she could feel the tears coursing down her cheeks.

And Sandy was saying funny things.

"That's it . . . That's the way . . . That's better . . . Go on. Get it all out of you . . . Keep crying . . . Don't try to stop . . ."

And she didn't, because the sobs seemed to bring to the surface everything which she had been forcing down for years. It was like a cesspit yielding the foul contents of its depths. Brian's affair with the waitress had shocked her deeply, made her indignant, but now with this new clarity which was growing in her she could see *why* he'd had an affair with her. It had been her fault, rejecting him, keeping herself away from him, depriving him of his son, leaving him alone and unloved and uncared for for all that time.

Oh, she had a lot to answer for.

And there was more. She thought of Brian the day Sergeant Phimister and Constable Murray had come to ask him questions. It had all been a foregone conclusion. Maggie had seen the waitress on the bus. Others had seen him go behind the garage and then her follow him. And they'd seen him emerge alone. . . . He'd listened quietly to Sergeant Phimister and then he'd admitted what he'd done and they'd asked him to come with them. He'd gone without a murmur, and he'd turned at the door and looked at her and there had been such pity and love in his look. She hadn't recognised it then as being for her. It was funny how long it had taken for it to become recognisable now. And he had never said a word about why he had gone to the waitress in the first place, why he had been driven into her clutches.

He had quietly accepted the contempt which had been

heaped on him in court and in the press and in Glendarroch: the man who had been unfaithful to his wife, who had treated her without pity and without respect, and he had never once raised his voice in protest at the injustice of it all.

She knew now that he had kept silent to protect her, to save her from that contempt which he had taken for her. That knowledge had been in the back of her mind since shortly after the shock of him being taken away, but only now had she allowed it to swamp her and propel her back into a stark reality.

It had been her fault again. He had been left alone, deprived of the love and care which were his right, while she had lived her own closely contained existence, blaming him for depriving her of her womanhood when she saw now that it hadn't been his fault. . . .

The tears began to fade and she lay still. She sensed Sandy Wallace still sitting on the edge of the bed, and now her mother was there too. She looked at them through blurred eyes and shook her head.

"I've got a lot to answer for," she said.

"Yes," said Sandy. "You have. But don't blame yourself. The person to blame is the person you became after the hysterectomy. She's gone now. She's been around a hell of a long time, but she won't come back."

"But Brian."

"*He'll* come back. And you can go and visit him. Tell him what's happened. And you've got work to do, Isabel. You've got a son to bring up and you've got a shop to keep. For Brian."

She nodded slowly.

"Jimmy?"

"He's downstairs," said her mother. "Do you want to see him?"

"Yes. Oh, yes."

Her mother went away and Sandy straightened the bedclothes and patted her shoulder.

"You're going to be all right now," he said.

He sounded confident and she hoped he was right, but there was an awful lot to face and an awful lot to do and there were ten years to get through before she could make adequate reparation.

She wiped her eyes firmly as she heard Jimmy's feet on the stair.

Chapter Four
1970-1974

1

The hall was echoey and almost empty. Under the canopy formed by the staircase the band from Auchtarne seemed limp and lifeless, perhaps because of the lack of response from the guests.

There were so few of them now, Elizabeth thought as her father stood holding the band's one microphone and made his usual New Year speech, welcoming the new decade. There had been no speech and no tot of whisky in the servants' hall this year either. There were virtually no servants left. Syme had gone to a job at Duff's garage in Auchtarne. John and Peggy had been given notice. Mrs Syme still came to do the meals each day. Only Archie Menzies lived in.

Father has shrunk, she thought, and he has become stooped. His Highland evening dress scarcely seemed to fit him any longer. The kilt hung untidily because he had had to pull it in a few notches in order to prevent is slipping down, and the shirt collar was far too wide.

And there were so few listening to him, too. No Strathmorrises. He had died inevitably of cirrhosis last June and she had gone to stay with their daughter in Cheltenham. The Honourable Arthur, now Lord Strathmorris himself, was trying to pursue a political career in the south and probably, she thought, remembering the smooth plausibility of the man, making a great success of it. And old Astrid MacAulay, the last of the Letir-Falloch family, had become a total recluse and was never seen outside the walls of the house.

Father finished his speech and there was a thin scattering of applause. The band burst noisily into an eightsome reel, an unwise choice, she felt, for there were scarcely eight guests capable of performing it.

She went to help her father as he moved away from the

microphone. He looked grey and drawn.

"Think I'll go to my bed, my dear," he said. "Not much point in staying on and being a death's head at the feast, is there?"

"Nonsense, Dad. There just aren't many of the old gang left."

"No. That's true. Oh, well. Try to get some younger ones for next year, Elizabeth. Liven the old place up again, dammit. It's getting to be like a morgue."

She helped him up the stairs and along the corridor towards his bedroom. The music faded behind them. From here it did sound like a masque of death.

"Fiona asleep?" he asked.

"I sincerely hope so."

"Let me have a look at her."

They were passing Fiona's door which stood slightly ajar so she quietly pushed it open and beckoned him in.

The light from the corridor spilt across the bed. Fiona lay with half the bedclothes on the floor, one arm flung round a slightly battered teddy bear.

Elizabeth replaced the bedclothes and she stirred but didn't waken. Her father stood looking down at her, his face shadowed because he was turned away from the door. He put down a hand and clasped one of Fiona's shoulders gently.

"Getting a damned big mouse, isn't she?" he whispered.

"She's going to be eleven."

"I know. I know. Good God, do you think I don't . . .?" He released Fiona's shoulder. "Good night, big mouse," he said more to himself than anyone else, and turned and left the room.

Maybe next year, thought Elizabeth, she should let Fiona see the New Year in. That would please her father.

Though she wondered whether next year there would actually be a New Year Ball.

2

When the call came that a man was missing on Ben Darroch and a search party was being organised Strachan knew he had no alternative but to go. He hated these occasions. It was one of the few times when he didn't feel in control of his actions.

He took one of the estate Land Rovers and drove grimly to the rendezvous at the path end which led to the southern slope of the ben.

It was a quiet, still March day, cold, but not freezing, and even as he drove he saw the grey cloud cover lowering over the peak.

He shivered, but not with the cold. There was something about this mountain which frightened him, brooding, solemn, uncaring. . . .

Sergeant Phimister and Constable Murray had rounded up a large search party in a very short space of time. The daylight would begin to fade in a couple of hours, maybe earlier if the cloud continued to thicken and the rain began. It was not long in which to search the ben.

They set off in parties of four and he found himself in a group which contained two locals from Auchtarne whom he didn't know and young Jack Campbell who must have been home on leave again.

There was something about Campbell which always made him uncomfortable. It was the way Campbell looked at him speculatively, as though each time their eyes met he was trying to seek a point of recognition. And there was something else, too . . . Campbell had appeared very quickly at the time of Lachlan's death. He must have been hovering around fairly close. Strachan sometimes wondered with some misgivings how much of that last conversation Campbell might have heard. He didn't think there was much in it that anyone could make a great issue out of, but he couldn't be sure in retrospect exactly what had been said. He'd taxed Lachlan with knowing a great deal more about the McBains than he had ever admitted. Perhaps he had gone so far as to accuse Lachlan of having made away with McBain. He had, he told himself, simply been baiting Lachlan, teasing him, trying to make life as difficult and uncomfortable for him as he could because Lachlan's stubborn refusal to give up the croft in spite of the pressure which had been put on him had set back Strachan's financial planning a

long way. Lachlan had flown into a towering rage, one such as
Strachan had not believed the man to be capable of. And that
rage had obviously caused his collapse and death. He
remembered the fury behind the words, the way the face grew
brick red and the body as tense as a coiled spring, as Lachlan
had finally given vent to all the pent-up hatred he had felt for
Strachan. He remembered his own shock when Lachlan had
suddenly stopped, choked and crumpled. It wasn't that he
cared what happened to Lachlan. If the man died, well and
good. But for him to do it out here on the hill with no other
witness than himself was really very inconvenient. It had been
some minutes after Lachlan's collapse that Campbell
appeared, but there was no knowing precisely what Campbell
might have overheard.

They climbed fast. The two Auchtarne men were clearly used
to the hill and Campbell, of course, was built like his father only
about six inches taller, tough, solid, rock-hard, ice-blue eyes
which missed very little, a dangerous man to cross . . . Strachan
found himself hard put to keep up with them and once or twice
they had to stop to wait for him, saying nothing about his
slowness, simply giving him a polite chance to catch up. Their
lack of condescension made him angry.

They moved into the cloud cover at about six hundred feet
and from then on they kept close together. The other three had
to mend their pace to his which was beginning to flag now. He
wasn't used to this sort of exercise and already his knees were
turning wobbly, his back was sore and his breathing laboured.

The going began to get rougher. What had started as coarse
grass turned rocky and the grass disappeared. They moved
from four abreast to single file as the route narrowed and the
others put him in the middle to nurse him. He wondered how
on earth they expected to find the man in this wide expanse of
broken rock and gullies, but the leader called and listened,
called and listened, and there were answering distant calls from
other parties, but none from the man they were looking for.

The dampness began to seep into him, stiffening muscles
which were already stiff. Damn it, why didn't it seem to affect
the others, he wondered, as he watched with some envy the ease

of their movements and the lack of concern for the physical discomforts they were facing.

He had no idea how high they had climbed when there was a distant shout from their left. The leader listened intently, but Strachan couldn't make out what was said.

"They've got him," said the leader. "He was on his way down and he's all right. The idiot should have left word when he expected to get back."

He looked at his watch and glanced round at the writhing damp mist.

"We'll take five before we start down," he said, and he sat down on a boulder and felt in his pocket for a bar of chocolate. The other Auchtarne man and Jack squatted down beside him.

Strachan looked at them with some envy. They seemed at home here, efficient, self-contained, masters of the situation. All he wanted himself was to get down to the path end and back to the Big House in the estate Land Rover as soon as he could. He began to move down the hill. Jack glanced up and saw him.

"Better stick together, Mr Strachan," he called.

"Back in a minute," he said.

In a second the mist had swallowed them though he could still hear their voices.

After he'd relieved himself he didn't turn back to where they were sitting. He began to move down the slope, and after a couple of minutes he wished he hadn't. On his own the mist seemed thicker and now the voices had disappeared and he was truly on his own.

He took off his glasses and wiped them. When he put them back on again it didn't make any difference. The mist was just as thick.

He should have stayed still and shouted. But he didn't want to lose face. He wanted just to stroll back into the group as though nothing had happened. He began to cast around for the way back and in a couple of minutes he was totally disorientated.

There was a shout from some distance away and he turned in the direction it had come from. It had been there . . . No, there . . .

He took a step and his foot slipped on a loose stone. He went over on his ankle and found himself falling. He cried out as pain lanced along his leg and then he was smothered in a welter of movement and noise until he was brought up with a jarring thud against a rock which drove all the breath from his body.

They found him a couple of minutes later and they worked efficiently and fast. He heard them talking to each other, quietly, urgently, and their main concern seemed to be that darkness would be falling in less than an hour.

"Joey's got the stretcher," said one of the Auchtarne men. "Lucky they didn't need it . . ."

"I'll stay. You get them up here fast," said Jack Campbell.

There was no argument. The other two men slipped away and disappeared into the mist and the sound of their footsteps faded almost as fast.

"Careful!" Strachan gasped as he felt Campbell working at his boot. Any touch down there caused him agony.

"You've broken it, I think, Mr Strachan," said Campbell.

"Just a sprain —," he said, trying to sit up.

"It's more than that. And don't try to move. You're lying very dangerously. There's a drop to your left. Lucky that rock caught you or you'd have been over."

Strachan turned and looked to his left. The ground seemed to stop two feet from his eyes and he stared into a swirling grey mist. His stomach heaved.

"I think you've bruised your ribs, too, so you'd better not move anyway. Charlie and Alastair have gone for the stretcher. They'll be back in ten minutes."

He suddenly realised why his vision seemed blurred. It wasn't simply the mist.

"My glasses," he said.

"I'll have a look for them," said Campbell, and Strachan heard him move away.

He didn't want to be left alone, but at the same time he didn't want to display weakness and ask him not to go away, so he gritted his teeth and clenched his fists, trying not to think of that yawning pit on his left.

A minute later there was a distant shout. He heard Campbell

answer, and then he appeared with Strachan's glasses.

"They're coming," he said. "Here are your glasses. I'm afraid one of the lenses is cracked."

He held them out to Strachan who reached up a hand to take them, but they were suddenly withdrawn and Campbell's face appeared fairly close to his own.

"That's who you are," he breathed. "I've got it now, seeing you without the glasses."

Strachan held his breath, feeling suddenly very cold. It wasn't from the long exposure to the dampness of Ben Darroch.

"One of the Glasgow evening papers . . . It must be fifteen years back . . . Just after my first voyage . . . There was a photograph."

Campbell had made a most unfortunate connection.

There was another shout, much closer, and Strachan knew he hadn't got much time.

Campbell gave him the chance. He got to his feet to answer the shout and Strachan found he could reach an ankle.

He grasped it and pulled as hard as he could. . . .

Campbell's yell diminished and then cut off suddenly. Strachan thought, a little sickly, that he could hear the thump of Campbell landing far below.

They reached him two minutes later with the stretcher, several of them, giving him time to work out his story. He gabbled hysterically about Campbell missing his footing and going over the edge and be quick for God's sake, they had to find him. He saw them look at each other and he knew by the expressions on their faces that they didn't think there was the slightest hope. He prayed that they were right.

It was a pity, he thought as he lay back and felt them start to lift him on to the stretcher while some others went off to organise a new search.

Campbell still had his glasses.

3

Dr Wallace stopped his car beside them and wound down the window. He took one look at the pale, shaking man clinging to her arm and said, "What are you doing out here, Mr Mack?"

"We're going for a walk," said Mrs Mack.

"I can see that," said Wallace grimly.

"He is very much better, aren't you, Hector?" said Mrs Mack. Mr Mack smiled and nodded but said nothing. "It's such a beautiful day that we thought fresh air would do him good, didn't we, Hector?"

"Yes, dear," said Mr Mack huskily.

Wallace got out of the car and came round to look at Mr Mack. Three weeks ago he had been summoned by Mrs Mack at two o'clock in the morning to find Mr Mack with what she described as a bad cold, which he had had for two or three days and she'd given him beef drinks and rubbed his chest with Vick but it didn't seem to make any difference.

Wallace had been impatient at being dragged from his bed in the middle of the night to drive to Glendarroch for something which should have been attended to a couple of days before, but had found the man breathing with difficulty and a bubble in his chest which had seemed ominously bronchial. After examining him he had realised why. He had suggested hospital, but Mrs Mack had refused, saying that she was quite capable of looking after her husband, thank you, a great deal better than those flibbertigibbets of nurses in the Auchtarne Cottage Hospital, and she wouldn't think of it.

He had argued, trying to explain that treatment was constant and specialised, but she was adamant, so eventually he had done what he could to make Mr Mack comfortable, had told her to keep him indoors since the weather was treacherous just now and hoped the man might have enough resistance to pull through.

He'd been back each day, expecting an improvement, but he had found none. He'd left instructions as to what she was to give him to eat but, looking at him now, he doubted whether they had been carried out.

What he hadn't bargained for was this sudden bright spell of April sunshine, nor on the fact that she would think it would do him good.

"We'll get him into the car and into hospital, Mrs Mack, if you don't mind," he said.

"Nonsense, Doctor, there's nothing the matter with him that a breath of fresh air won't cure —"

"Stop arguing, woman! This has gone on too long," he said sharply and she gaped at him indignantly. He helped Mr Mack into the back seat and ordered Mrs Mack to join him and then he drove as fast and as smoothly as he could to the Cottage Hospital in Auchtarne and arranged for Mr Mack's admission.

He forgot about Mrs Mack while Mr Mack was taken to the side ward and put to bed in a hospital nightshirt. He only thought of her again when he was on his way out to continue his interrupted visits and she came out of the waiting room in a cloud of indignation and faced him.

"Really, Doctor, I must protest at this high-handed treatment," she said.

"If you have any protests to make, Mrs Mack, you can put them in writing and send them to the health board. But I'd be obliged if you'd get out of my way and let me get on with my work."

"And how am I to get back to Glendarroch? You brought us here against our will."

"There's a perfectly good bus leaves from the station yard in about half an hour's time. But if I were you, I wouldn't think of going back just yet. I'd stay and make sure that your husband's all right before you go."

He pushed past her and left the hospital.

Later in the day, after his evening surgery, he returned and found her sitting beside Mr Mack's bed. Mr Mack was propped up on pillows, his eyes closed, an oxygen mask over his face and an intravenous drip attached to his arm. Wallace picked up the chart at the foot of the bed and examined it.

"He's not saying anything, Doctor," said Mrs Mack, and

there was now a note of worry in her voice. A pity it hadn't been there several years ago, he thought.

"That's hardly surprising," he said. "He's suffering from malnutrition which has left him so weak that he has no resistance to something which he should be able to throw off in a day or so."

"I'll have you know he has had the best of attention since we were married, Dr Wallace. I have slaved for him every minute of the day."

"If you had let me take him into hospital last week he would have been all right," said Wallace, hanging the chart back on the bottom of the bed.

"What do you mean — *would* have been —?"

Wallace looked at her with little sympathy.

"I've got a nasty feeling we've got to him too late," he said.

The day faded outside the windows and a nurse came and switched on the lights. Outside the door the sounds of the hospital continued, muted and seemingly distant.

A little later the eyelids fluttered and Mr Mack took a deep breath. He seemed to want to say something. Wallace removed the oxygen mask, but before Mr Mack could speak he was interrupted.

"Can you hear me, Hector?" demanded Mrs Mack.

Wallace thought he detected a sigh, but it might just have been a fight for breath. Mr Mack's lips moved without effect and then he tried again.

"Yes, dear," he whispered.

"You see? He's all right," said Mrs Mack. "There was absolutely no need to bring him in here, and you can take that ridiculous thing out of his arm. I shall take you home tomorrow, Hector, and I shall make you a strong cup of beef tea —"

"Yes, dear," said Hector and closed his eyes for the last time.

4

"That's your supper in the oven, Mr Cunningham. I'm away."

"Right, Mrs Gilligan, thanks," said Peter.

"See you tomorrow."

The door slammed shut behind her. Peter poured himself a gin and tonic, took it to one of the seats in the window and sat down. He sipped his drink as he looked out over the park in which the children were playing a simplified form of cricket.

He felt strangely at peace and contented.

That was odd. He hadn't seen Elizabeth or Fiona for about eight weeks. And he had to admit that of the two he was actually missing Fiona more than he was missing Elizabeth.

He would miss her even more in September when she went off to St Leonard's. Elizabeth had had her own way over that, as she'd had her own way over most things, which may have been one reason why he enjoyed the peace of the flat with no one to bother him except Mrs Gilligan who came in each afternoon when he was at the office and stayed to cook him a meal in the evening. There was something to be said for the freedom of a bachelor existence again.

Yes, he would miss Fiona, and he hoped she would miss him.

There was no doubt, though, that the marriage was breaking up, he thought gloomily. But it had done so gradually, without heat, with the minimum of fuss and in a civilised manner. It was just a parting of the ways, one to Glendarroch, the other to Edinburgh. And it was probably irretrievable.

There had been pain, of course. He was still very fond of Elizabeth, and he believed she was still very fond of him, but their lives were too diverse for easy living together.

But it was a sort of limbo. And he wondered, as he picked up the gin and tonic again and watched someone's stumps flattened in the park, how long it could go on like that.

5

She caught sight of the deckchair as she stumped up the drive to the Big House. There was a canopy over it, keeping the June sun off the head of the occupant, but she could see who it was.

She veered off the drive and headed for the deckchair.

Sir Logan sat there, a blanket round his knees, a white hat on his head. His eyes were closed and he seemed to be asleep, but as she approached he opened them and stared at her.

"Who are you?" he asked.

"I want a word with you, Sir Logan," she said.

"Do you indeed? Who are you?" he repeated.

"I am Mrs Mack as you know perfectly well."

"Mack . . . Mack . . . Oh, yes. The old Thomson cottage . . . Your husband died, didn't he? Sorry about that."

"It's not about my late dear husband that I wish to speak," she said.

"It isn't?"

"I wish to complain in the strongest possible terms about this new rent rise."

Sir Logan sighed and closed his eyes again.

"I'm afraid you'll have to see my factor about that. Mrs — er — what's your name? — Mack? He handles these things."

"That's not good enough," she said. She sensed that Sir Logan was not very strong, so automatically she began to assert herself. "Where is the money to come from, may I ask?"

"That's a very good question," murmured Sir Logan, without opening his eyes.

"And I have to warn you that if you insist on raising the rent then I shall not renew the lease of the cottage —"

"That's your privilege —"

"Mrs Mack. What are you doing here?"

She turned round and found herself facing Mrs Cunningham. Suddenly she found the domination she felt she had established over Sir Logan dissipated, but she continued to try to exert her authority.

"I am complaining about the rent rise, Mrs Cunningham —"

"Then please do so to the proper quarters. My father is not to be bothered with such things, do you understand?"

Mrs Mack puffed indignantly and then turned and strode off down the drive and out of the gates, quivering as she went. How dare that woman talk to her like that!

But she'd told Sir Logan. The lease of the cottage expired at the end of the year. After this new rent rise she had made up her mind that she would not renew it. That would show them. They'd have an empty cottage, and it wouldn't be easy to let at the new rate. Serve them right.

She headed for the manse, wishing to find someone to share her indignation with, and for want of anyone else Lizzie would do.

Lizzie was washing the lunch dishes and Mrs Mack clicked her tongue. It was half-past two in the afternoon and that was a job which should have been done an hour ago.

"Is this as far as you've got?" she demanded.

"Please don't start, Mary. I know I'm awfully behindhand, but there's been such a stramash today —"

"There always is when you have anything to do, Lizzie. Give me that towel and I shall finish these for you . . . Och, look at that plate! You haven't washed it at all. And egg. Have you been giving the minister egg for his lunch?"

Lizzie clutched the edge of the sink and bowed her head.

"I've told you before you will make the man egg bound. It's very, very bad for him—"

"Stop it!" Lizzie suddenly shouted shrilly at the top of her voice, and she picked a plate out of the sink and smashed it on to the stone floor of the kitchen. Mrs Mack looked at her open-mouthed. She had never seen such irresponsible behaviour in Lizzie before.

"Lizzie!" she said.

"You made me do it. It was your fault. I wish you'd leave me alone —!"

Mrs Mack looked at her sister grimly, and as she did so her course suddenly became plain.

"That is the last thing I am going to do," she said. "Listen to me, Lizzie. I am leaving Glendarroch."

Lizzie looked at her, almost hopefully, she thought.

"You are?" said Lizzie. "When?"

"Very soon. I never wanted to come here in the first place, but what with you and my dear Hector —"

"Poor wee man," said Lizzie softly.

"He is beyond pain and suffering now," said Mrs Mack.

"Yes. He's lucky."

"And when I leave Glendarroch, Lizzie, you are coming with me."

Lizzie looked at her, not quite taking it in, and then her eyes widened in horror.

"No!" she said at last.

"Yes. I cannot leave you here on your own. You are far too irresponsible. We shall go back to Glasgow and you and I and Florence will live together just as we always used to."

"I can't —"

"You can and you will. I insist."

"But the minister —"

"The minister will just have to find another housekeeper locally. There shouldn't be any shortage of applicants."

"Mary, I can't — I can't — !"

"No can't about it, Lizzie. My mind is made up. You will give the minister a month's notice today and we shall leave immediately after that notice has expired."

6

"Where's my mouse?"

"She's at school, Dad."

"Ah. Yes, of course. Forgotten about that."

He was disappointed, she could see. He lay in the big double bed in the big bedroom with the big dark mahogany furniture. It all made him look very small. There was a single lamp burning on the bedside table.

He seemed to be breathing evenly and shallowly and he was quite obviously not in any sort of pain. He is an old man, she thought. He would have been eighty on his next birthday.

She thought he had fallen asleep, and she was about to call Dr Wallace, who was waiting outside, but he suddenly swallowed and opened his eyes again.

"Sorry I'm leaving you a bit of a mess, Elizabeth," he said.

"Don't be silly, Dad," she said, feeling the tears trying to force their way out of her eyes. She was not aware of any mess, and she bitterly regretted not having paid more attention to the actual business of running the estate. It had been an integral part of her life, and she had deserted Peter for it, but all that hadn't impelled her to find out anything about how it all worked. She had been content with the romantic, unconcerned with the practical. And now she would have to find out from Strachan, and she wasn't sure whether she would get the full and accurate story from him, and the thought of having to co-operate with him filled her with dismay.

"You'll look after it, though," he said.

"Of course I will."

He nodded briefly.

"Perhaps Peter will help you . . ."

She said nothing, because there was nothing to say to that except things which would upset him and she didn't want to do that.

"Perhaps," she said at last because he was looking at her, waiting for some kind of response.

He lay silent for a long while, but she could see that he hadn't left her yet. The hand which she held was still firm in hers, but his eyes were staring sightlessly at the ceiling as though he were wondering what else there was to say, what final message.

"Give my love to my mouse," he said at last and his voice was little more than a whisper.

"Of course I will," she said.

He nodded as though he appreciated the fact that she hadn't protested insincerely that he would see her at Christmas in a few weeks' time. He knew and she knew exactly what the situation was. He wouldn't see the New Year Ball . . .

"I'm sorry there wasn't a boy, though," he murmured.

They were the last words he said. A minute or two later he slipped gently into unconsciousness and she called Dr Wallace who came quietly to his bedside.

Sir Logan Peddie died at 4.31 a.m. on the morning of Thursday 12th November 1970.

7

Mrs Mack looked grimly round the cottage. It was all going to have to go, she thought. The van was coming in the morning to clear the furniture and would take it to the saleroom at Auchtarne.

That much was definite. The cottage had to be cleared by the 31st December. What happened after that she was not entirely sure. And that worried her.

She wouldn't have come back here anyway. Not now when she would have to go to that woman at Glendarroch House and beg for a renewal of the lease. It would have been bad enough going to ask Sir Logan for it, but certainly not that stuck-up Mrs Cunningham.

The trouble was that she had burnt her boats in Glasgow now.

Maybe she had been hasty, but she couldn't possibly have gone on living with Florence. Florence had always been the flighty one of the family. Mrs Mack had forgotten just how flighty. Florence laughed too much, took nothing seriously. If she wasn't out at some party where strong drink was available she was content to sit at home in the evening, never thinking of attending the church soirées, never devoting her life to the things that mattered. Many times Mrs Mack had come back and found her and Lizzie sitting watching half-naked chorus girls cavorting on the television screen in the living-room, and when she had remonstrated Florence had merely laughed again. That was simply one symptom. She had eventually had enough and told Florence that unless she was prepared to mend her ways, stop playing loud jazz music on the wireless first thing in the morning, give up the *Daily Record* and subscribe to a more cultured paper and, in fact, to undertake an altogether more sober existence, she, Mary Mack, her sister, would be forced to leave.

And Florence had agreed! It was unbelievable, but Florence had not been in the slightest bit put out, and even Lizzie had seemed to take Florence's part. Mrs Mack got the impression that both of them believed that they would be better off and happier without her.

Well, she would show them. She had declared that after the New Year she would leave them together, believing that that ultimatum would bring them to their senses. But they hadn't protested, they hadn't broken down and begged her to stay as she had expected they would, and the unfortunate result was that now she had nowhere to go.

She was here to clear out the cottage and when that was done she was on her own.

Not that that worried her. She had no doubt that somewhere in this wide and wicked world there was work waiting for her to do. The trouble was finding it. And finding it quickly, because the sands were running out.

She earmarked all the goods in the cottage, which of them were to go to the saleroom, and that included much of the rubbish which Hector had brought from his mother's house in Auchtarne, and which were to go into store until such time as she had another home she could use them in, and then she made her way to the manse to pick up one or two things which that flibbertigibbet Lizzie had left behind when she left the minister's employment.

It was a long time before anyone answered the bell, and eventually it was Mr MacPherson himself who came to the door. She was shocked at his appearance. The man had put on weight and his clothes looked shabby and unkempt.

"Mrs Mack," he said. "Do come in, please. I have put Lizzie's possessions in the hall here, but perhaps you would care to look around in case I have missed anything."

She did so and was even more shocked at what she found. She had thought that Lizzie kept a very untidy kitchen, but now it was indescribable. The dust was thick on the mantelpiece and you could hardly see out of the windows. The kitchen table could do with a good scrub. There were dirty dishes piled in the sink and she sighed and took off her coat and set to to wash them. There wasn't any hot water so she put on a kettle to boil some.

While she was working the minister came in and saw what she was doing.

"This is very good of you, Mrs Mack," he said. "I'm afraid I am not much of a housekeeper."

"Evidently not," she said.

"Mrs Haggerty comes in once a week to try to stem the tide," he said, "but I fear she is somewhat slapdash."

She snorted. She knew Mrs Haggerty, a poor slatternly body with a thriftless, drunken husband and several very dirty children. She wouldn't have allowed Mrs Haggerty over the doorstep. She picked up the frying pan from the cooker. It was full of congealed fat and the remains of a sausage and it was badly burnt on the outside.

She clicked her tongue and scraped the remains out of the pan into the refuse bin which was already overflowing. On the dresser she found a biscuit tin with its lid off. It was full of chocolate biscuits. Really, that was too much!

She faced the minister firmly.

"This will not do," she said.

"I fear there is no alternative," he said. "Since my wife died I am afraid domestic arrangements have proved a little too much for me."

"Someone must take over," she said.

"Indeed, but who? Mrs Haggerty does her best, but —"

"Mrs Haggerty will have to go," said Mrs Mack. "You need a proper housekeeper."

"Yes, but —"

"Well, you have found one, Minister. The Lord has obviously guided me to you in your time of need. You are extremely lucky, but as it happens I am free to undertake the job."

"But —"

"No buts. I shall start immediately after the New Year."

He protested, but she would have none of it. The man quite clearly needed her. She needed somewhere to live. The two things were providential.

Mrs Mack had found her mission in life.

8

There was no New Year Ball, of course. It would not have been right so soon after her father's death, but she wondered whether there would have been one even if he had survived. She had gone so far as to check through the old guest list. There were very few left that she would have invited now.

Things seemed to be changing very fast and uncontrollably. On this last evening of the old year, she was alone in the dining-room with the two George Carradines, not in the hall with the band and the tartan and the old friends. This was not exactly a celebration as the New Year Ball had always been. More a sort of wake, especially in view of what old George was saying.

"I very much fear that death duties will be substantial," he said.

"How much?" she asked.

"It's too soon to say, and I shall put off finding out for as long as possible, because there is no doubt that we shall need time to pay. If we can get it."

The shadows which had been round them since they had sat down in this huge, echoing room seemed to draw closer and more menacing. Really, the three of them sitting here was absurd. She would have to think about closing up part of the house, making it conform more to the style of living which she had learnt in Edinburgh and which she was feeling more and more she would have to introduce here. All she and Fiona needed was three rooms. . . . She sat at the head of the long table, where her father used to sit. Old George sat at her left-hand side and young George at her right. The rest of the table disappeared into the gloom beyond the candlelight, and she shivered suddenly.

A way of life was drifting away into that darkness, never to be recalled.

The house was very quiet. There ought to have been a band playing, people talking and laughing. Now it was empty apart from the three of them and Archie Menzies clearing up in the kitchen and Fiona asleep upstairs. Mrs Syme would have gone an hour ago, her work finished when the meal was served.

"I did advise your father to make over the estate to you as a gift at the time of your marriage, but he was reluctant to do so."

"Do you know why?"

George Carradine fingered the stem of his brandy glass and avoided her eye. He was eighty now, she knew, and yet his spare frame was upright and his eye was as bright and observant as ever it had been.

"I think he felt that perhaps Peter was not the right man to take over the estate," he said.

On her other side young George stirred uncomfortably. She nodded, wondering if perhaps her father hadn't shown more foresight than she had done herself.

"But a lot of trouble could have been avoided. He would have had to live for seven years after making the gift in order for it to be free of death duties. Perhaps he felt he wasn't likely to live that long."

"But he did."

"And more."

"He may have been right about Peter. Well, what do we do now, Mr Carradine?"

"Hold tight in the meantime and pray for a miracle," he said drily, and the shadows seemed to draw closer at his words.

9

Maggie laid her teacup down on the counter with a clatter.

"There are things happening on this estate which I don't like, Isabel," she announced.

Isabel took the cup and refilled it from the pot behind the post office counter.

"What makes you say that, Maggie?" she asked.

"That Mrs Cunningham. Do you know what? She's stopped my pension. The one her father paid me ever since my father died."

"Why is she doing that, do you know?"

"She said she knew nothing about a pension."

"Well, I remember you telling me that he was paying it out of his own pocket."

"That's beside the point. She said all sorts of things about the estate not being able to afford it, but I think it's just meanness, that's what it is."

"I don't think you can accuse Mrs Cunningham of being mean, Maggie."

"Oh, can't I? She isn't one of us, Isabel, that's the trouble. Married that man from Edinburgh and went off with him. There were years when we hardly ever saw her. Now it's all broken up and she's come home with her tail between her legs, and she doesn't know anything about any of us. What's worse, she doesn't care."

"Oh, yes, she does care. Just the other day she brought Jimmy home. She'd found him wandering along the road after school, not wanting to come back here. He was crying and he'd got a black eye and he'd obviously been in a fight."

"Boys will be boys."

"Oh, I know that. But she cared enough to take him up to the Big House and clean him up. She gave him some tea, and he and Miss Fiona played hide and seek, she told me."

"A stuck-up little madam, that."

"She doesn't seem that way to me."

"You see too much good in everyone, Isabel."

"No, I don't," she said, thinking of someone she had seen no good in for far too long. "But the point is, I know why he got into a fight. He gets teased at school. Told his father's a murderer."

"Well, so he is."

Isabel grimaced, feeling the hurt inside her. Maggie was nothing if not direct.

"What worries me is what's going to happen when he starts at the Auchtarne High in August. It's going to get worse for him there."

10

Mr MacPherson placed his knife and fork together with a sigh of contentment. The main course had been plain but beautifully cooked and there was plenty of it, something which he found he didn't get at the manse. And Mrs Cunningham had really made a very pleasant job of this first-floor wing of the Big House, turning it into a comfortable, warm flat.

He looked round the company at the table. Peter Cunningham sat at the foot, and Mr MacPherson was glad to see him there. He didn't come to Glendarroch very often and the minister hoped that everything was all right with the marriage. He had heard rumours and he had to admit he had had doubts himself. On his left sat Dr Wallace and opposite was young George Carradine.

The last hours of 1971 were slipping into oblivion and the feeling that change and decay were all around grew strong in him as it always did at this time of the year, leaving the familiar old year and facing the unknown new one.

And the talk had been of change. He had sat listening while Peter and George Carradine explained that the estate was in a parlous financial condition. Peter had actually said that it was moribund and Elizabeth should get rid of it while she still could, and Carradine had backed him up. Mr MacPherson had listened with some dismay, hoping that saying this wasn't the only reason for Peter's visit, to tell his wife that her life lay in ruins. But he knew that things were not healthy on the estate, that there would inevitably be a heavy bill to pay for Sir Logan's death, but the way the two legal gentlemen were talking filled him with a certain alarm.

In a break in the conversation he cleared his throat deprecatingly.

"I have been listening to what you have been saying," he said and stopped.

"Go on, Mr MacPherson," said Peter Cunningham.

"Well, you have spoken at some length and with a great deal of common sense about the financial problems of the estate.

You have dealt with the facts and figures and profit and loss, I am sure very effectively. I am afraid I am no expert on these matters. But I am somewhat concerned that in all you have said you have missed out one very important aspect."

He glanced round the table and saw Peter Cunningham and George Carradine looking at him in surprise.

"You haven't mentioned the people," said Mr MacPherson.

He heard Dr Wallace grunt beside him, and it sounded like a grunt of approval, and he noticed that Mrs Cunningham smiled encouragingly.

"You see, the estate is people, far more than houses and fields and crops. Oh, houses and fields and crops are a part of it, but people are a part of it too, and I think it would be unwise to divorce one from the other."

"But we are concerned about the people, Mr MacPherson," said George Carradine.

"Oh, I'm sure that's true, but I wonder whether, coming from the town, you truly appreciate the way in which the people here are a part of the estate and the estate is a part of the people. Now, as I understand it, you are recommending that Mrs Cunningham sells off the estate. I notice you don't suggest who to. Suppose — and it's pure supposition, believe me — that you sell the estate to a man who wishes to turn everything over to the rearing of sheep. As I have no doubt you know, that *has* happened in the past. And the people suffered then. Now, for sheep you may substitute many different things. Marinas, holiday camps, and I'm sure there are other ideas being dreamed up by the purveyors of desirable holidays. Any of these would affect our people. And that is the point of my concern. You can't sell off the people, you know. I'm sorry. I'm not putting this very well. But each Sunday I see them from the pulpit. *Our* people."

"It's not the people who are the millstone round Elizabeth's neck," said Peter Cunningham. "It's the whole thing. This vast, unusable house which costs a fortune in rates let alone upkeep. The days have gone when anyone can keep something like this going. It's become a white elephant. I appreciate your worry about the people, but there is no reason to believe that they will suffer. A change of ownership won't make any difference to them. They'll still be born and marry and get ill and die, isn't that so, Doctor?"

Wallace nodded.

"Yes," he said. "That's the common lot for all of us, even round this table."

Mr MacPherson sensed that the doctor was administering a slight rebuke.

"But Mr MacPherson's right," said Wallace. "You can't treat them as you can a house or a field or a few sacks of oats."

"You're advocating this antiquated feudal set-up should continue?" asked Peter.

"I'm not sure about any of it," said Wallace. "It may be antiquated, which doesn't mean it's bad. It may be feudal, though I think you're misinterpreting the concept. And I don't know whether it should continue. I just think that Ian's right. You have to think of the people as people. Not as things."

"Thank you," said Elizabeth. "I feel we've cleared the air and I'm grateful for your help. Before we move through for coffee, may I sum up? It seems that two of you are advocating selling the estate. Two of you are advocating keeping it. That means I have the casting vote. Well, I've cast it. I'm keeping it."

11

The smoke from the chimneys blew into tatters in the strong March air. In the summer you couldn't see the Big House from here, but now she could make out the roof through the bare branches of the trees. Beyond it all, the loch lay mottled with waves and it lightened and darkened as gusts of wind blew across it.

Elizabeth stood on the hill and looked down on the village. It was eight weeks since Mr MacPherson had spoken about the estate being people. What he had said had crystallised her views and it had also galvanised her into activity. Since that time she had moved round the estate, meeting the people, talking to them, hearing their problems, discussing their work, growing closer to them as her understanding of them grew.

She was, she believed, now beginning to think as her father had thought. She had learnt what she should have learnt earlier instead of going to Edinburgh to live amongst the legal set. "Look after the estate" was almost the last thing her father had said to her and she had promised him that she would.

Somehow it had to be made safe for them all.

It would mean hard work, work which unconsciously she had started the year before when she had closed off the top floors of the house, all except the wing which she had kept and converted into a flat for her own use. That cut down on some of the costs. Not much, but it was a step in the right direction. The servants' quarters and the kitchen premises were now closed, and the factor's office moved to the old morning-room. There was no need for them now.

It had been hard and heartbreaking to make these changes, but they had to be done and she knew that there would have to be many more before she could herself hand on the estate to Fiona in her turn.

And at the back of her mind was the continuing worry.

Where did Peter fit in to all this?

12

Fiona loved the summer holidays when she was free for days on end to do what she liked when she liked, and this year the weather had been lovely for day after day.

There was, of course, the slight fear of the unknown at the end of it, because in a few days she would watch all her school friends take the bus to the Auchtarne High School while she stayed on her own until September and then get taken across to the other side of the country to St Andrews and school at St Leonard's. The thought of a new school amongst new people she'd never met before was the one slightly dark cloud on her horizon.

But now everything was absolutely perfect because Daddy had come for a month's holiday and would be here till it was time to take her to St Leonard's.

She wished he came here more often, but she knew that work kept him very busy in Edinburgh and it wasn't easy for him to get away. She was very pleased to see him and so was Mummy. At least, Mummy said she was.

But shortly after his arrival Fiona began to be aware of funny things happening. When she burst into the room in which they were talking very quietly together the conversation would stop immediately. There was a funny sort of feeling in the air when they started to talk again rather loudly about what she was doing and was she enjoying herself and would she like to go anywhere or do anything in particular. It was as if that wasn't the important thing they had on their minds.

There was one day when she found the door of the sitting-room in the flat ajar, so she opened it without making any noise and she heard Daddy say:

"So *you've* got nothing now, and *I* certainly can't afford these fees. So what are we going to do?"

Mummy's face was a bit red and she opened her mouth to say something but caught sight of Fiona in the doorway and she smiled rather suddenly.

"Hallo darling," she said brightly. "Where have you been?"

She told her she'd been playing hide and seek with Jimmy Blair but Mummy didn't really seem very interested. Neither did Daddy, and soon afterwards she'd left them to go and play in the garden by herself. Archie Menzies, who was the only other person left living in the house now, had promised to help her to build a tree hut.

Then there was the night when she awoke in her room. It was very dark and she had no idea what time it was. It must have been the voices which came from the bedroom next door which had woken her, and she listened to them drowsily, not understanding them, but knowing that they must be talking very loudly for her to hear them through the thick walls.

They were arguing. And as she listened, not able to make out actual words, but hearing the tone of their voices, she realised that this was the same sort of thing she had interrupted at other times only worse.

She swallowed and turned over and drew the sheet and blankets over her head, trying to blot out the sound because it worried her, made her feel frightened and insecure, and she wanted it to stop.

The next day Daddy said he had to go back to Edinburgh. She was very disappointed because she had been looking forward to going up to the home farm with him and taking the pony out on the hills.

He picked her up at the front door and hugged her hard. Then he put her down and looked at her very solemnly.

"Fiona," he said, "supposing you had to make a choice, which would you choose? To live in Edinburgh or to live in Glendarroch?"

"Oh, Glendarroch, Daddy, of course," she said immediately and he nodded.

"I thought you'd say that," he said. He looked at her for a moment and she thought his eyes were very sad. Then he bent and kissed the top of her head. "I'll be back to take you to school, Fiona. Be a good girl, now."

And then he got into the car and drove off without looking at her again and she wondered why he wasn't going to come back until it was time to go to school.

And there was another funny thing. Mummy hadn't come out to say goodbye to him.

13

Grace was in a bit of a fluster. It wasn't every day that the lady laird came to see you.

Mrs Cunningham sat at the kitchen table, sipping the cup of tea Grace had made her. It was strange how quickly people had come to think of her as the lady laird. She was very like her father, thought Grace, though probably a bit more approachable than the old laird had been.

She had come unexpectedly that morning just after Dougal had gone out on the hill after his breakfast and she'd asked if Donald kept accounts.

"Oh, yes, Mrs Cunningham, he was always very particular about that," she'd said.

"Do you think I might have a look at them, Mrs Lachlan?" Mrs Cunningham had asked, and Grace had hurried through to her bedroom and turned everything upside down trying to find the things. She'd put them away after Donald died two years ago and had forgotten about them. She found them at last at the bottom of a drawer, old, dog-eared, the pages splotched with ink blots where the nib of Donald's pen had protested on several occasions. Donald's writing hadn't been very good.

And now Mrs Cunningham was sitting at the table going through the account books and Grace was wondering why. Had Donald done something silly which he'd never told her about? What reason was there for Mrs Cunningham to come and look at them? Surely that was the factor's job if there was anything wrong, though she had to admit it was more comforting having Mrs Cunningham in here than the man Strachan.

"Do you know if these are accurate, Mrs Lachlan?" she asked, and Grace grew more worried.

"I'm sure they will be, aye, Mrs Cunningham," she said. "Donald was always very careful with money. Not stingy, you understand. Just careful."

"Yes, I remember," said Mrs Cunningham, and she turned a page, squinting at the writing as she tried to read the scrawl.

Grace hovered, not very sure whether to help her with a decipherment, but decided it would be better not to.

"Is there something wrong?" she asked at last, unable to contain her anxiety any longer.

"I'm not sure. I sincerely hope not. Tell me, did Donald always pay things by cash?"

"Oh, yes. I never could persuade him to open a bank account. Well, that was natural, I suppose. Living away up here it's difficult to get to a bank and you sometimes need cash in hand. I kept telling him it would be a good idea but he put off and put off. I had an awful job getting Dougal to open an account. Why, it's only in the last year or so I've been able to use our best teapot again — "

Her voice trailed off because Mrs Cunningham wasn't listening. She closed the account books carefully and piled them on top of each other.

"Put these away safely, Mrs Lachlan," she said. "We may need them and I wouldn't like them to disappear."

"Are you sure there's nothing wrong?"

Mrs Cunningham smiled suddenly.

"Certainly there's nothing for you to worry about," she said. "Leave the worrying to me."

She finished her cup of tea and rose to go. Grace accompanied her to the door and watched as she drove the estate Land Rover up the track and disappeared over the brow of the hill.

Then she turned back to the croft house, wondering what on earth all that had been about.

14

Strachan was sitting at his desk in the morning room when she walked in. He rose to his feet politely and smiled at her with his mouth.

"Mrs Cunningham, good morning," he said. "I thought you had gone out."

"You are quite right, Mr Strachan. I have been out," she said equably. "Now I'm back. Could I have a look at the estate accounts, please?"

She was watching for it and she saw the momentary look of anxiety cross his eyes behind the glasses.

"The estate accounts?" he asked.

"That's what I said. The estate accounts."

"Oh, dear. I'm very sorry, but I'm afraid I haven't got them."

"You haven't?"

"No. They are with the accountants."

She looked at him levelly for a moment and then picked up the telephone and dialled the estate accountants in Auchtarne, watching him while she did so. The look of anxiety had changed to one of something resembling alarm.

"Mr Hamilton, please," she said when the girl in the office answered. "Mrs Cunningham, Glendarroch House."

There was silence as she waited and she stared at him. His eyes gave before hers and he sat down again and busied himself with some papers on the desk in front of him. At least, he shifted them around a bit and held one of them up as though he were reading it, but she didn't think he was taking much of it in.

"James Hamilton. Good morning, Mrs Cunningham. What can I do for you?"

"Good morning, Mr Hamilton. I wonder if you could tell me if you have the estate accounts with you?"

"Hold on a moment and I'll check."

There was silence again. She stood holding the receiver and watched Strachan who seemed to be studying the bit of paper even more closely.

"Mrs Cunningham? We don't have the accounts here, I'm afraid. I expect you'll find that Mr Strachan has them."

"Thank you, Mr Hamilton. Sorry to have troubled you," she said and replaced the receiver.

She stood without moving or saying anything until he was forced to look up from his paper.

"The accounts aren't there," she said.

"How odd. I posted them a week or two ago. Really, the postal service is getting very slipshod, isn't it? They may have got lost."

"It seems strange to post them when they only have to go to Auchtarne," she said. "I expect you'll find they're still lying around somewhere here. I'd be grateful if you would look for them and let me have them as soon as possible, Mr Strachan."

She turned and left the office without looking back.

15

George Carradine wished his father was here to listen to what Elizabeth was saying, but the old man had finally retired at the age of eighty-one and taken to fishing, a simpler pursuit, he maintained, than dealing with the legal problems of Auchtarne.

"That's a pretty serious allegation, Elizabeth," he said. "Can you substantiate it?"

"I remember my father saying that Donald Lachlan came to him after church one day and produced some involved story about being put out of his croft. Father pooh-poohed the idea because he was more worried about mother at the time. It was only a month or two before she died. But later we all became aware that Donald was very worried about his holding, and we couldn't think of any reason for it. He knew as well as anyone that crofters have security of tenure. You remember that Donald died of a heart attack while he was talking to Strachan on the hill."

"I remember that."

"He hadn't been well for some time, I believe, but I sometimes wonder what was actually said at that time to bring on the attack. Then there was the business of Jack Campbell."

"He was lost in an accident, wasn't he?"

"Yes. During a rescue in which Paul Strachan got injured. Jack Campbell was with Strachan when he apparently slipped and fell down the *coire nam Fuaran*. It seemed a little odd at the time. Jack Campbell was very sure-footed on the hill."

George looked at her in astonishment.

"That was recorded as an accidental death, if I remember," he said.

"Yes."

"Elizabeth, you're not going to start a did he fall or was he pushed thing, are you?"

"Well, it worried me at the time and it's worried me even more since. Old Jock was pretty cut up about it, not unnaturally, and Ina died shortly afterwards, but Jock has always maintained that Jack had recognised Strachan, though Jack couldn't remember how or where he'd seen him before. Jack dying in that accident has always seemed terribly — pat to me, George."

"Elizabeth, I hope you know what you're saying."

"I know exactly what I'm saying. And I wouldn't dare say it

anywhere else but here. Anyway, there have been enough straws in the wind to make me wonder. And so I went to the Lachlan croft two weeks ago and asked Grace if Donald kept accounts. Fortunately he did. I examined them."

"And what did you find?"

"I found that Donald was consistently paying out a great deal more in rent than appeared in the estate account books. He paid in cash, as they all do, of course, and guess who collects the money? Strachan. Now, none of the other crofters are as methodical as Donald. They don't keep accounts so there's no way of checking, but it seems that all of them have been paying more than the estate has received, and it looks as though Donald Lachlan may have been paying a great deal more. I think Strachan and my father agreed to raise the rents. It has to be done periodically, as you know, to keep pace with inflation. But I don't think my father ever checked to make sure that the rent rise which they agreed was actually the amount which was being paid. I have the feeling that Strachan has been bleeding the Lachlans dry."

"You can't prove any of this."

"No, I can't. But I've asked Strachan for the estate accounts and he keeps putting me off. He's put me off for three weeks now, and I've no doubt that he will eventually produce them when he's had time to cook them so that the discrepancies can't be spotted."

"It's all very vague, Elizabeth. You haven't got a case that would stand up in court."

"I know that too, George. But what's worrying me is this. If Strachan has been bleeding the crofters he may well have been bleeding the estate as well. And from what you say about our financial position, that's the last thing we can allow to happen."

"So what do you want me to do?"

"I want to find out about Strachan. Why does he need this money so desperately that he's willing to take these excessive risks? Neither you nor your father was involved in his employment, were you?"

George shook his head.

"I thought not. So that means the only people who might know where he came from, what his background was, are my parents who are both dead. And possibly Old Mackinlay who died five years ago. There is no one left."

"That's true."

"As you say, there is not enough evidence to inform the police. But you must know of some enquiry agent, George. Get them to find out about him. Find out what Jack Campbell knew about him and may have been stopped from telling us. If we know more about him we may have a hold which would give us a chance to recover some of the money which may be missing."

"I don't like it, Elizabeth. I'm very reluctant to employ an enquiry agency. Some of your hypotheses seem pretty wild to me."

"George, I want him investigated as quickly as possible. And that's an instruction."

16

"We've reached the crossroads, haven't we?" said Peter, and Elizabeth looked at him, knowing exactly what he meant.

Outside the window of the flat the trees fringing the loch were bending with the force of the October gale, and the leaves were rioting down, leaving the branches stripped and bare. The turmoil out there matched the turmoil she had felt since he had arrived unexpectedly that afternoon.

"It's over a year since you've been to Edinburgh, you know," he said and guiltily she had to admit that that was true. She hadn't realised just how quickly time was passing. "People are beginning to talk. Mind you, they've been talking behind my back for a long time. Now they're beginning to talk to my face. Offer me advice. I don't like that."

She said nothing because she didn't feel there was anything she could say, simply crouched in her seat, staring at the logs crackling in the fire.

"It's time you came back, Elizabeth."

She shook her head.

"I can't. There's too much to do," she said.

She heard him sigh. But what she said was true. There was this Strachan business, apart from the whole question of trying to look after the estate. She hadn't realised what a full-time job it was.

"In that case I think we ought to agree to separate," he said so quietly that it took a second or two for his words to sink in.

When they did they came as a relief rather than as a surprise but she looked up at him with a feeling of great sadness welling up in her.

"You mean divorce?" she said at last.

"It seems the only way out, doesn't it?" he said with surprising gentleness. "You won't come to Edinburgh. I couldn't stay in Glendarroch. What else is there for us?"

"There's Fiona . . . ."

"She's at school. Maybe you were right about St Leonard's. She's away from any hassle there. And it won't be a messy business, will it, Elizabeth? I mean, we're both sensible, moderate, intelligent people."

She turned away and looked back into the fire, her eyes unfocused through tears.

"Victims of circumstance," she said tritely.

He came and put a hand on her shoulder and she put a hand on his and they stayed like that for a long time as the short dusk gathered in the room.

17

The sheets were closely typed, evidently on a very old machine by someone without much training in the art. George Carradine looked up from them and smiled a little grimly at Elizabeth.

"I have to apologise for doubting your wisdom," he said. "This is the enquiry agent's report."

"They've uncovered something?"

"They've uncovered a great deal. I'll get a photocopy of this for you, but I'll give you the gist of it now. Briefly, Paul Strachan was jailed for three years in 1956 for bigamy."

"Bigamy?" said Elizabeth in astonishment, wondering how any woman could have fancied this man, let alone two.

"Yes. He has two wives and five children to support. They are all of school age and the wives apparently both believe in private education, so he is quite clearly in desperate need of money. There is your motive. A photograph of him appeared in the Glasgow *Evening Times* on the day of his sentence, and we can assume that it was that photograph which Jack Campbell saw and failed to recognise. I have checked with the port authorities and found that Jack's ship docked at Greenock the day the photograph was published, so it is quite possible that he saw the paper. There is a copy of the photograph attached, and you can see that it is not a very good one."

He handed it over and she looked at the slightly fuzzy newspaper cutting of a man being hustled out of court, one hand half hiding his face, and she wondered whether she would have recognised it herself. The man was very much younger, of course, and he wore no glasses, and the surprise was that Jack Campbell had actually had that face fixed in the back of his mind at all.

What had happened to Jack?

She shivered as she laid the photograph back on the desk. They would probably never know, and it might be as well if they didn't. Better that Jack should remain the hero that he had become locally, the man who died trying to save Strachan from death on the mountain.

"Can we take him to court?" she asked.

George shook his head dubiously.

"Certainly not for murder. There is no evidence at all, and besides you would merely be opening old wounds for Jock Campbell. Better from our point of view if folk are allowed to go on thinking that he simply died a hero's death on the hill, don't you think?"

It was exactly what she had thought herself, though it went against the grain to allow Strachan off with anything.

"I doubt if there's enough evidence even for embezzlement," he said. "It would be touch and go, I think. You might not win, and then you'd have the costs of the case to meet. And whatever the verdict you won't get back the money which you believe he may have milked from the estate."

"Don't you believe the story, George?"

"As a person I believe it. As a lawyer I have doubts."

"So no court case," said Elizabeth, getting up from her seat. "I shall just have to try to deal with the man myself."

He looked at her with grave concern.

"If your hypothesis is right you may be dealing with a murderer."

"I know."

"Be careful."

"Oh, believe me, I shall be."

18

Elizabeth stood with her back to the morning-room fireplace. She still thought of it as the morning-room rather than the factor's office, perhaps because she didn't like to give it the designation which assigned it to the man who was sitting at the desk in front of her.

There was silence between them. He looked quite calm, but she could tell that he was shaken by what she had said. She had told him of her suspicions about what he had done to the crofters, the Lachlans in particular, and she hinted at what she thought might have happened on the hill the day Donald Lachlan died. She had also, in passing, mentioned the name of Jack Campbell.

"You have any evidence of all this?" he asked at last quietly.

"None whatsoever," she said, matching his tone, "because I really haven't had the time to look for it. But I have no doubt it is there somewhere. I'm simply hoping that it won't be necessary for me to start a search."

He smiled.

"I'm very sorry if I have lost your confidence, Mrs

Cunningham," he said with the customary oil in his voice.

"You can't lose what you've never had," she said.

"What do you intend to do?" he asked.

"Well, that's the problem, isn't it? Your contract still has four years to run."

"That is true."

"I can't break it without good reason, and finding that good reason would involve me in a lot of work, as I've said. I'm not sure, for the sake of many people's peace of mind, whether that would be a good thing. If, however, I am forced to undertake it, I shall do it very thoroughly and I am quite sure that many other things may come to light which I have no knowledge of at the moment."

He looked away and she could see that there were beads of greasy sweat on his forehead now, although the room was not very warm. There was snow outside and a high wind forced its way through gaps in the window frame.

"There is another way, of course." He glanced at her quickly, almost hopefully. "There is nothing to stop you from resigning," she said, and silence fell in the room again.

19

He had no car of his own and George Carradine stood beside Elizabeth in the factor's office and watched Strachan walk down the drive on his way to catch the bus to Auchtarne. He had given Elizabeth a month's notice and now he had gone.

She could think of no one who would regret it. Already she had the feeling that there was an unspoken conspiracy to wipe his name from their memories. With luck very soon no one would even remember his name.

"I feel as if a shadow has been lifted," she said.

"One shadow has been lifted, another one falls, I'm afraid," he said.

Elizabeth turned away from the window and sat down at the desk. There was something symbolic in that, he thought. She had finally assumed the position of power. It was a pity it was too late.

"I was pretty sure you hadn't just come to wave goodbye to Strachan, George," she said.

"No. Hamilton and I have been through the accounts."

"Tell me the worst."

"I'm very much afraid it's just about as bad as it can be. There's a lot of money missing."

"Strachan?"

"Undoubtedly. And none of it will be recoverable. The man is bankrupt. As is the estate, virtually."

"Damn him," said Elizabeth.

"By all means," said Carradine, "and I'm sure it will do your feelings good to do so, but it would be unwise to put the blame entirely on him. Hamilton and I are of the opinion that he has merely hastened an event which was virtually certain in any case. You may remember two years ago my father and I warned you of this situation. The disappearance of this money is, I'm afraid, only a fleabite. It has hastened the end by perhaps a week or two. No more."

She seemed to turn pale as he spoke and he wished he didn't have to say it. It went against the grain to hurt her in any way, but it was as well she should know the truth now rather than be left to find it out in dribs and drabs later.

"What do we do?" she asked after he had stopped speaking and they had sat in silence for some time.

"Two things, I think. First, you must find a good, honest factor who can see you through the difficult months ahead."

"And second?"

"Sell the estate."

20

"I should warn you that the estate is up for sale and so there may be no security in the job," Elizabeth said.

She had thought a lot about what George had said that day and finally, after a few weeks, she had come to the conclusion that he was right. There was no other course left open to her. The estate would have to go.

It was a grim concept. What would she do? Where would she go? There had been Peddies at Glendarroch for as long as recorded history. They had no other home, no refuge in which she could hide to lick her wounds. She knew that all things come to an end, and that the end had begun when her parents had not produced a male heir, but she was herself still a Peddie. Fiona was half a Peddie and there would have been continuity. And there was no guarantee that a male heir would have been able to stem the tide . . . Oh, Peter, Peter, if only our roles had been reversed. If you had been the son and I simply your wife, what a difference that might have made! But styles of life changed, not always for the better, and she had to bow to circumstances. It had taken her a long time to accept this, but she had done so now, not willingly, not happily, but with a philosophical realisation that it was inevitable.

But she had not wanted to employ a new factor. It seemed presumptuous to believe that anyone would take on the job simply to assist in selling off the estate and immediately thereafter find themselves out of work again, but eventually she had realised that she needed someone to look after the business, to ensure that the estate was at its best and most active to impress any prospective buyers, so that she might get as high a price for it as possible. If she had to go down she would go down in style with all guns blazing.

So this was the third prospective factor she had interviewed today and there were three more to come. Of the first two one had been too old and too ill and the other had shaken his head regretfully when she had said that the estate was up for sale. She could understand his attitude.

This third man was tall and good-looking with a quiet, competent, confident air about him. She took to him as soon as he walked through the door into the factor's office. But, she thought, first impressions could be deceptive. Look what had happened with her father and the man she was still trying to forget. This applicant was dark with a moustache and he looked bronzed as though he had spent some time in a hot country.

His name was Alan MacIntyre.

"I understand that, Mrs Cunningham," he said in reply to her warning. "I assume, though, that whoever buys the estate will need a factor. They might not have a spare one of their own."

She laughed.

"What have you been doing up till now?" she asked.

His original home was the north of Scotland but he had recently been manager of an estancia in Brazil where they had also bred horses.

"That sounds exciting," she said.

"It was very hot."

"You like horses, Mr MacIntyre?"

"Very much."

"What made you leave Brazil?"

A shutter seemed to come down over his face, though he remained courteous.

"Personal reasons," he said pleasantly, though his tone forbade further enquiry and she respected it.

There was a clatter outside the window which grew louder and a helicopter dropped towards the lawn, hovered and then came to rest. Elizabeth looked at her watch.

"He's early," she said. "Trust a German."

"A prospective factor in a helicopter?" said Alan MacIntyre. "I didn't expect such competition."

She answered the twinkle in his eyes with a smile of her own.

"No, not a prospective factor, a prospective purchaser," she said. "He wasn't due till twelve o'clock. Now, what am I going to do with him till then?"

"Would you like me to take him off your hands for a couple of hours?"

She looked at him speculatively, wondering whether this would be wise. But the arrival of the helicopter so soon left her little alternative.

"It'll give you a chance to see your other applicants. I don't expect you to chalk it up in my favour," he said with a brief smile.

She made up her mind.

"That's very good of you, Mr MacIntyre," she said. "His name is Max Langeman and he's a big tycoon with a vast business based in Frankfurt and several million marks behind him. I don't know any more about him than that."

"It's certainly an impressive start. He speaks English does he?"

"Very well indeed."

"Thank goodness for that."

He left the office and a moment later she saw him walk across the lawn to meet the man who had just emerged from the helicopter.

She interviewed the three remaining applicants and as she was winding up the last one she heard the clatter of rotor blades start up and a moment later the helicopter rose from the lawn.

The final applicant, a somewhat weedy youth straight from university, left and a few minutes later Alan MacIntyre reappeared.

"How did you get on?" she asked.

"Fine. I showed him round the house and the policies and the village. He seemed quite impressed."

"How could you do that? You don't know Glendarroch." He smiled again.

"I did a bit of homework before coming here," he said.

"Would you like the job?" she asked.

"Yes."

"Then you've got it," she said and wondered if any job offer had ever been concluded so quickly before.

21

"My parents' divorce is through," said Fiona.

She sat on the edge of his desk, wearing a bottle green polo necked pullover and jodhpurs. He knew she had had the pony out on the hill for a couple of hours after lunch and he wondered what hurtful things had been going through her mind during that time.

"I know," he said.

She swung a leg, not looking at him, watching her shoe with intense concentration. It had happened at a bad time for her, Alan thought. She would be fourteen next month.

"Does it worry you?" he asked gently.

She didn't say anything, just nodded very briefly, still examining her shoe.

"That's good," he said. "It should. It shows you care."

She turned and looked at him.

"It's happened to you too, hasn't it?" she said and he blinked at her unexpected insight. He'd never said anything about his personal affairs, but Fiona needed comfort and this might be one way he could help her.

"Yes," he said.

"You're divorced too?"

"Yes."

"Why?"

"That's always a very difficult question to answer, Fiona. My wife's father owned the estancia I was managing. I think to her I was more of a servant than a husband."

"Is she Spanish?"

"Yes."

"Was she beautiful and sultry and did she have a terrible temper?"

"Yes to both questions. And I wanted to come back to Scotland. She didn't."

"It would be cold for her."

"Brazil was hot for me."

He sat back. It was getting dark outside now and very soon it would be Christmas. He thought of putting on the desk light but decided not to, though there was still a lot to do. Strachan had left an appalling mess behind him and he hadn't got it all straightened out yet. It took longer when he found he couldn't ask about his predecessor. It was almost as if there was a taboo on his name. But he felt this conversation was very important to Fiona and he didn't want to cut it off by switching on the light.

There was silence for a long time and when she spoke again it seemed as though she had accepted what he had said.

"Have you sold the estate yet?" she asked.

"I'm not sure. I think so."

"Only think?"

"Yes. I may have laid down too many conditions," he said.

22

"All I can say, Isabel, is that it obviously doesn't pay you to win a war," said Maggie as she lifted the mug of tea which Isabel had just put down for her. "I mean, your father was killed by them. My father was gassed by them. Sir Logan himself fought against them. And now they're coming here to take over the estate and drive us out of our homes and no one seems to be prepared to do anything about it. I'll tell you this. Sir Logan would be turning in his grave if he knew about it."

It was surprising to her how calmly Isabel seemed to be taking the latest news.

"But there's nothing definite yet, Maggie," was all she said.

"There's no smoke without fire, you know that as well as I do. He comes here in that helicopter of his and goes snooping around looking at people and not saying anything to them, just as if they were cattle at the market. I don't trust Germans."

"Well, I can't say I've any reason to like them," said Isabel. "But I'm quite sure Mrs Cunningham wouldn't do anything wrong."

"Huh! That's what you think. I don't think Mrs Cunningham's got any control left now. I think the estate's been allowed to go to pigs and whistles. And what I want to know, Isabel, is this. If this German takes the place over what's going to happen to us?"

23

"I knew how keen you were to protect the people in Glendarroch," said Alan, "and I've done my best to ensure their safety."

Mrs Cunningham sat opposite him in the factor's office. Outside, the spring sunshine was slanting low across the lawn and shimmering off the loch. She was looking out of the window at that view, not looking at him at all, though he knew she was listening. He could understand that. That view out there of the policies and the loch and the hills was what they were talking about.

"And do you think you've succeeded?" she asked.

"I hope so. It's been a tough couple of months, but I think I've done as well as we could expect. Here are the broad details of it. I'll go over them with Mr Carradine later. Max Langeman will buy the estate through a company which he will set up for the purpose."

"And what does this company plan to do with the estate?"

"That's being left vague at the moment, but I'm pretty sure his idea is development."

"You mean a yachting marina? Holiday cottages? Caravan sites? That sort of thing?" she said with extreme distaste.

"Things like that are not barred from the agreement, but I understand that at the moment he is thinking more in terms of setting up shooting parties for his rich German colleagues, which means that they won't make too much difference to life as it is just now."

"Except for the deer."

"There are too many of them, anyway. They need to be culled. But I'm not sure how long he will be content with such an arrangement, or indeed how long he would be prepared to foot the bill for something which is unlikely to show him very much financial return. The main point is that this company he is going to set up will have a board of nine directors, of which he and four of his nominees will form part."

"And the others?"

"One of the others will be yourself, and you will have the power to nominate three others of your choice."

She turned and stared at him.

"You persuaded him to do that?"

"Yes. It wasn't easy."

"It can't have been. You've done miracles, Alan. I'm most grateful."

"It won't give you a controlling interest, of course, but it does mean that nothing can happen without your knowledge, and if anything is proposed which you object to very strongly you can advise against it, try to dissuade and if the worst comes to the worst be downright obstructive so that they will find it very hard to push things through against your wishes."

"That will be a great relief."

"And in view of your position on the board you will have the right to go on living in the house."

"The Big House? They're not going to turn it into a hotel?"

"Not at the moment, no. And I think once they've got to know the place that idea will become less attractive. No, it will be owned by the company. But it will still be your home."

"For Fiona later?"

"Yes."

She stood up suddenly and turned for the door where she stopped with her hand on the handle.

"There will still be Peddies at Glendarroch," she said with a slight break in her voice. "Thank you, Alan. Thank you very much indeed."

And she went out quickly without looking back.

24

They were waiting in the factor's office. Beyond the window the trees were frozen into stillness and the loch was a smooth metallic grey against the lighter grey of the lowering sky.

George Carradine was there. And his father, sitting close to the fire and still wearing his overcoat. His eighty-three-year-old frame needed protection against the winter. And Alan

MacIntyre. And Fiona. And herself. There were empty coffee cups on the desk, and she cleared them absently away, returning them to the tray.

The others would be here any minute. Germans were always punctual.

"I won't be long," she said.

She took the tray out of the office and put it down on a table in the hall. Her coat hung on the hall stand and she put it on, opened the glass door and stepped out on to the porch.

The cold struck her as soon as she was outside. It was piercing, and matched her mood.

She walked across the gravel drive on to the lawn and down towards the loch.

It was changing. To all intents and purposes it had already changed.

When she reached the shore of the loch she turned and looked back at the Big House, its windows and roofs and turrets grey and matt brown against the darkening sky.

The house had been built by her great-grandfather on the site of an older house which itself had been built round a fortified tower which went back to the dawn of history. Through those years, she told herself, much had happened. If those stones were sentient things the new change which took place today would probably not affect them at all. They would scarcely notice.

She had, she remembered with a shiver, bathed from this point in the loch when she was very young. She hadn't done it often because the water was bitterly cold and her mother had eventually put her foot down when she came out one afternoon a delicate shade of blue. There had been teas on the lawn, and just over there had been the marquee which her father had had put up for her wedding reception. Where was Peter now? she wondered. She'd asked him for the New Year but he'd refused gently, perhaps feeling that it wasn't the time for him to be present when the transfer documents were being signed, saying to her simply by his presence, "I told you so". She appreciated his tact but she missed his support.

To her right the smoke from the chimneys of the cottages in

Glendarroch rose into the still, biting air. They would be safe, thanks to Alan MacIntyre. And in the hills the crofters were safe anyway with their built-in security of tenure. On the surface nothing had changed at all. But for how long would all this last?

Whatever had happened in the last year or so, she knew that this would not be the end of Glendarroch. It would change again, maybe not for the better, though perhaps that belief was simply a sign of advancing age.

The sound of a car horn pierced the chill of the air and she heard the scrunch of wheels on the gravel.

Elizabeth Cunningham shrugged herself deeper into her coat, shrugged off the bitter-sweet memories as well, and walked back towards the house to welcome the New Year visitors.